The Dark Half of the Year

North Bristol Writers

The Dark Half of the Year

Published by North Bristol Writers
In association with Iande Press and Far Horizons
Trade paperback edition 2016
Edited by Ian Millsted and Peter Sutton

ISBN 978-0-9554182-2-8
Printed by Ingramspark

Contents

Introduction *Cavan Scott*	5
This Is Me *Kevlin Henney*	7
Guten Rutsch! *Desiree Fischer*	11
The end of British Summertime *Ian Millsted*	23
Burnton Cary *Roz Clarke*	33
Twelfth Night *Peter Sutton*	59
Tom Bawcock's Eve *Chrissey Harrison*	72
The Ancestors *Dolly Garland*	85
The Raven's Death *Ian McConaghy*	103
Empty Chairs *M E Rodman*	113
Your Honest, Sonsie Face *Ken Shinn*	119
The Last Four in the Bar *Madeleine Meyjes*	136
Vallum Hadriani *Justin Newland*	143
Dark Time *Clare Dornan*	148
Love and Christmas *Thomas David Parker*	154
Retribution *Suzanne McConaghy*	164
Epiphany *Margaret Carruthers*	176
Winternights *Maria Herring*	177
Love Is a Stranger *Nick Walters*	191
About the Authors	209
Acknowledgments	215

The Dark Half of the Year

Introduction

Cavan Scott

Why do we read ghost stories?

We read them to be afraid; to know fear from the comfort of our favourite chair, or tucked up safely in bed. Nothing can hurt us. Yes, so our hearts may beat that little bit faster and our skin may crawl, but we're the ones in control. We can shut the book at any time. We can return to the real world whenever we want. To the safe world. *Our* world.

So, we keep that light on. We pull the curtains and take care not to glance at the mirror that we pass it in the hall, but we know that there's nothing waiting in the darkness, nothing watching from the bottom of the stairs.

Nothing standing over us as we sleep.

Ghost stories remind us that not everything can be explained. They talk of regret and hope; fear and wonder. They reveal the secrets we hope to forget, and the loves that we long to remember.

They never explain, but suggest. Never answer, but question. They challenge and tease. They force us to see the world from the corner of our eye.

There are stories in this book that will unnerve. There are stories that will shock. Some will turn your stomach. Other's will break your heart.

You will find yourself lost at sea, hunted by ancient gods, and trapped in a single moment of time. You will experience things that you know should not exist, and wonder if the dead ever dine with the living. You will see friends facing fears, and lovers taking revenge. You will travel to the past and into uncertain futures.

You will be scared and you will be haunted.
And you will ask one simple question...
What if it happened to me?

Cavan Scott
November 2016

This Is Me

Kevlin Henney

Shoppers find their way to the shops, the market and the shopping centre through crowds, traffic and twilight. Some find their way to buy that special gift, others that casual gift. While some track down the last few items on their list, others have only just begun, last-minute panic setting in, as winter's chill sneaks past gloves and scarves. Couples use the chill as excuse to hold tighter. Children find warmth against it through grasped mittens.

You take my right hand.

Winter's chill has an edge, an edge both softened and sharpened by the onset of Christmas, an edge cut on the blade of the longest night. That edge is softened in the air by mulled spices, roast chestnuts and sugared excess. But it is sharpened in the shadows. There is more to winter's chill than can be told by any thermometer. Those couples holding together? Those grasped, mittened hands? It's for more than love, for more than temperature.

Everyone needs to hold on.

But there are those who can't. Those who do not have that someone special at the other end of the gift. There are those who are lost. And those who have lost. Lost that someone they held, or whose mittens they grasped.

You squeeze my hand and look up at me, asking, "Can we go now?"

"Are you sure?" I say. "Have you seen enough? I don't think we've seen all the shops; there are some new ones since last year."

"I know... but they're the same, really, aren't they? They never really change, do they?"

The shops and the shoppers change with time only in the way rivers change with the flow of water. I smile. "Shall we head back, then?"

"Yes."

We walk, the same route every year, away from town along roads lit by car-light, each car different, each the same. We switch between silence and short-lived exchanges about what we pass as we walk. As we approach a crossing there is a car unlike all the others.

Reflex has me pointing, saying, "Look." Pointing to its difference. Pointing before realising. But too late. We both look.

The hearse slows. It anticipates the lights before they change, ensuring it does not separate from the black cars behind it, ensuring it does not pull its too-small coffin any further from parents who must already feel a distance between *what is* and *what might have been* that no heart should ever travel.

As we stand, waiting for red man to become green, I feel small fingers reach to take my left hand. I look down. The child looks up at me, holding my hand, but unsure. You lean forward and smile at the child. You stare at each other.

"It's OK." You break the silence. "It's a bit confusing at first. But it does get better."

The child smiles back.

"Was it an accident?" you ask.

The child nods.

"Me too." You look up at me before looking back. "Car?"

The child nods again.

"Snap," you say. "I know I should have looked, that I shouldn't have run out like that. I know that. I knew that then. But... it's OK now."

The green man changes back to red — we missed this crossing — and the procession pulls away. The child at my left side is gone. I prefer silence as we wait for red and green to change places once again, knowing our destination is the same.

That edge of night cuts the veil between the worlds, between the real and the imagined; today the cut is at its deepest.

We arrive at the cemetery. Off the path to the left of the entrance, tears and words join funeral-black silhouettes barely visible against dusk, night falling to cover the too-small coffin as it waits by freshly dug earth.

We take the path to the right and walk a few plots, still in sight of the entrance.

"This is me," you say.

We stop by one of the newer headstones. Not as new as it used to be, but still loved and cared for. Fresh flowers sit by the base. And a small gift, newly wrapped and ribboned. The dates etched into the stone are not far enough apart. Too close for anything to be said. But the inscription tries. Its choice of words struggles to hold more than can ever be told in writing, struggles to hold back tears and more than a parent's heart can bear behind the front of chiselled brevity and taste.

You are held, timeless, at the end of those brief years. You are bound to me as I am to you, the tide of what happened drawing you over to me each year, when the breakwater between worlds is at its thinnest and darkness flows more easily into darkness.

You let go of my hand. If we had been friends or family this would be a parting of hugs and smiles, but we part without a wave, we part as strangers. I turn without looking back, knowing you will be gone but ever present for another year.

I walk on, further into the cemetery, paths that wander left and right, to and fro. Fewer souls come this way, where the plots are not as well kept, nor as welcoming. It was an accident, but my part in taking you from this world, its weight, pulled me from all who held me close. I had to be apart. From everyone.

I stop by a headstone. Simple and new — a little newer, but not as new as it used to be.

Beyond my dates and my name, there are no words, there are no flowers, there is no gift. This is me.

Guten Rutsch!

Desiree Fischer

You know when everything is so fucked you feel the only thing that could help would be if someone would come to save you? No? Well, that's just me then, I guess. Or me, not too long ago.

Another New Year's Eve. Another night full of empty promises and forgettable resolutions. I'd decided to stay in. My friends just wanted to get pissed, and, while I usually enjoyed spending time with them, I preferred them sober. Alcohol would often bring on a bout of devastating frankness that I could live without. I knew I hadn't progressed as much in my job as I should have in the last four years. I was well aware that I was still single and that every one of their friends they tried to set me up with became suddenly very busy after the first meeting. I knew I wasn't eating as healthily as I should and that my body wasn't in the shape it could be. But should that really matter? Instead of receiving all this judgement, I stayed home and played video games alone. I really didn't fancy company, not even the virtual kind. I could only endure my cat, Miss Pebbles, who usually ignored me anyway.

So I played an open-world RPG, running around the wild trying not to bump into too many NPCs, slaying whichever monsters were thrown at me. It wasn't even nine o'clock when I felt tired, despite my self-induced, gaming-and-cheese-ball orgy.

My dreams that night were funny, more so than my run-of-the-mill, monster-fighting ones. I was talking to my grandmother, who'd passed away five years ago. It didn't matter; we had a good old chat.

She'd always thought of me as special; close to her heart. She hadn't grown up in England, and scattered her speech with German expressions, assuming everyone would understand. When I was a young girl, running around full of dirt and my mother was having a headfit over it, she encouraged me with 'Recht so!' - *That's right!* When I was a teenager, falling out with friends at school, she hugged me tight and explained it was because I was special and while they could feel it, 'Sie wissen's halt nicht besser!' - *They don't know any better!* As a young woman, straight out of university, having spent three years doing what I love, taking pictures and exhibiting them, I was ready to take on the world but, even more, scared of it. She was in hospital, dying, but still encouraged me, reminding me that I could do whatever I put my mind to. 'Du schaffst das!' - *You can do it!* I had determination, she said, and that was vastly different to most – those who would go with the flow and never try to really achieve something.

Yet here I was, making ends meet at a dead-end job for which I was over-qualified for, even before university. And I wasn't taking photographs any more. Everyone takes pictures nowadays with their phones, right? So, was there anything of value I could offer, really?

"But you have determination," she said, her ball of wool rolling around in the little basket next to her as her knitting needles flew. She sat in her comfy reclining chair, as she always did, and I sat by her feet, looking up at her.

"Maybe I did, but I think it's gone."

"And where would it go to?"

"I don't know."

"Because it wouldn't just go. You need to stand back up and give it another try. Life is hard, believe me. I have experience. Who would think that you'd live as healthy as can be and you die of lung cancer? Never smoked a single Zigarette in my life, and that's not a lie. Never mind, but that is not the point here. The destination is not important but the journey is. What good is das Ziel if die Reise isn't lovely?

So what if you will never be the greatest photographer in the world? Should you just completely stop, even though it brings you joy? You don't like your job... change it then. Yes, I know it's scary. I know you'd have to get out there, apply and get rejected. I know you're worried that you will not make it somewhere else, but you'll never know until you try. As long as you have determination, you will always land on your feet, no matter what the situation. So what if it doesn't work out? Then you go on. Life is not a straight line; it's a web with many different directions."

"You're dead."

She looked at me sternly over her glasses. "So, instead of thinking about what I've said, you're just stating the obvious? Maybe you are right and your incredibly hard life so far has extinguished that spark of yours." Sarcasm dripped from her voice.

"No, I mean... Wait, you are aware that you're dead...?"

"Of course I am. How couldn't I be? Never been as high in my life as I was when it happened, but it happened alright."

"Oh." What does one say to that? I wondered if the additives in the fizzy drinks I had consumed over the day had given me weird dreams.

"Anyway, stop wasting your time and get on with it. In the end, we all end up at the same destination."

I opened my mouth to defend myself, but she ploughed on before I had the chance. "And don't forget to take a cookie before you go."

I shrugged, and took one of the square cookies stashed on her little crafting table, closing my eyes as I took in the familiar taste of my childhood.

When I opened them again, the image of my grandmother faded. She smiled and wished me a "Guten Rutsch ins neue Jahr." Before I could wish her the same - as apparently, even the dead celebrated the New Year - I found myself rubbing sleep out of my eyes. I was lying on my sofa, my controller vibrating in my hands. My game character was in the process of being killed. To my disgust, when I faced the TV, I discovered my cheek was covered in drool. I made a mental resolution to give up fizzy drinks for New Year's. I realised I had only nodded off for a few minutes. It wasn't even half-nine yet.

I ate more cheese balls and carried on with my game, keeping an eye on the clock, as it crept towards twelve.

As midnight approached, I put down the controller. I watched the hand slowly moving towards the twelve and I wondered what another mediocre year would bring. A few seconds before midnight, I got up to look out of the window, to see how much money people had wasted on fireworks.

I blinked as I heard the first firecracker going off and I heard a whisper in my ear.

'Streng dich mal mehr an!' - *Put more effort into it!*

To my surprise I found myself back on the sofa, complete with cheese puff crumbs, controller rumbling in my hand, my virtual head being chewed off by some mythical beast - again. I looked at the clock. It was just coming up to nine-thirty.

I was freaked. Was this a dream showing me that I was supposed to do better than staying inside, playing video games? Fine. I put on my jacket and pulled my trainers on. I would go and see what was happening.

Maybe I had just experienced a dream within a dream? No, that sounded too meta, even for me. It was probably a really good idea to go outdoors, just to make sure I was truly awake and it was still the same day, and that I hadn't done something stupid, like knocking myself out when I went to the window. Maybe this was my afterlife, and my corpse was doomed to be slowly eaten by my mostly-timid, but occasionally feral, cat.

The air was cool, but dry; surprising for a New Year's night. In my experience, it would usually rain, just to spite anyone who wanted to amaze the neighbourhood with their fireworks display. I wasn't keen on impressing people, nor was I easily impressed.

I went to the pub around the corner, too downtrodden to be ticketed for New Year's, and took a seat by the bar.

"What date is it?" I asked the bartender.

He didn't even throw me an odd look. Everyone around me was pissed out of their faces already. One of the fellas on the other side of the room was even wearing a traffic cone. So, my request didn't seem too unusual.

"Still the 31st, my dear. We haven't quite made it yet. Couple of hours to go." I nodded, and asked for a G&T. I decided to stay there to ensure I wouldn't nod off again and have funny cheese puff-induced dreams.

I watched the people in front of me getting progressively drunker, demonstrating all the possible things one could do with a traffic cone, even some that I had never imagined and frankly didn't need to see, and decided that I was probably not cut out for a career in catering.

But was I even cut out for my career? I was a receptionist for a building that housed a lot of small businesses. While I saw other people getting their promotions and pay rises, their nice new suits and designer bags to go with it, I was still on the front desk, in the same place for four years, in the same backache-inducing chair I had sat in since my first day. Back then I thought this would only be the beginning, now I know it was the end. The hours were horrid, the pay pitiful. How was I able to live with myself?

I squirmed at the thought. Maybe I just had to make it work. I couldn't deal with living with other people and their quirks, and I didn't like the idea of folks criticising mine. It wasn't even as if it was a bad job, just not for me. As with my relationships, my career and I had irreconcilable differences. I'm sure someone else wouldn't mind the hours or the pay and would use it as a stepping stone. I never could. I had hit a dead end.

A lot of the people in the pub were like the people I saw every day. Working hard, but also playing hard. I was doing neither. I glanced at the clock and New Year was nearly upon us, so I knocked back my fourth G&T, ready to leave, once all the hubbub broke out. Before I could go, a group of tweens asked me if I could snap a picture of them and I grabbed the offered camera. The weight of it stirred something deep within me. It had been months since I'd held a camera in my hands. They didn't really care how I took the picture, but I did. I made sure everyone was in the shot and that I caught the best side of them. They would thank me later.

I really wasn't in the mood for this forced joyfulness. Everyone turned to their designated New Year's kiss and I turned away in disgust and blinked, hearing a whisper of 'Echt, jetzt?' - *Really?* in my ear.

My controller was vibrating in my hand. Again. My head immediately snapped to the clock, taunting me with the time it was displaying. Game Reset. Yet again.

I was seriously rattled. This New Year's Eve was quite something... different. Once could be a dream, an odd one but never mind. Twice... was outright creepy. Whatever I was doing was still not good enough for my dear old nan. I had no doubt that this was her way of motivating me, even from beyond the grave. I knew she had been stubborn in life, but I hadn't realised she could be even more so in death.

I grabbed my phone and started taking pictures. Of me. Of the cat. I tried not to imagine the cat chewing down on my comatose body while I was stuck in this weird dream world. As I was just snapping photos with the phone, I felt a bit calmer. I liked to focus on the angle the light hit. I liked the way I could see every single hair on my cat's body. These phone cameras had really come a long way.

Taking the picture earlier in the pub made me realise how much I missed this. The measuring look before each shot, the click and the anticipation before I looked at it, hoping I had captured the moment, just how I wanted to. It was a satisfying process, one that relaxed me.

Miss Pebbles wasn't so relaxed. After a few minutes, she wanted to play with my phone, and thought I was pulling it away to play with her. Big mistake. My right thumb was adorned with a huge scratch only seconds later.

Sucking on my thumb to stem the bleeding, I absent-mindedly grabbed a plaster for it and thought about how I'd always wanted to take pictures of my city from the bridge. The fireworks would look great from that height. Then I remembered how, the day we had finally decided to go up there, my boyfriend Adam had broken up with me. He didn't even have the guts to say it to my face, just texted me when I was getting ready to meet him. Saying it wasn't me - it was him and he was sorry. Two weeks of depressing self-analysis later, I discovered that it was indeed him. Him and his secretary. My friends saw them having dinner with their parents at a fancy restaurant. I'd never met Adam's parents when we were together.

I looked at the clock and realised I must have been lost in my thoughts. It was already one minute to twelve.

"Let's see what's going to happen." I said to Miss Pebbles, keeping my eyes fixed on that relentless minute hand. I wouldn't let it happen this time. As the clock was about to click over to twelve, Miss Pebbles, having none of it, jabbed her paw into my face. I instinctively shut my eyes, and straight away in my left ear I could hear a demanding 'Jetzt aber!' - *C'mon!*

I opened my eyes, knowing what I would see:the same screen, still showing my imminent death-by-mythological-beast. It was nine-thirty. Again.

I decided I wouldn't let the year end with the image of my ex. still so fresh in my mind. I showered and dressed, up to the nines. Hair, make up, dress. Not the one with the sequins that I'd bought earlier this year, though. It had this intimidating aura around it. I felt that I had to earn the right to wear it.

High heels on. Ready to go. I grabbed my clutch bag and headed out, to a party I had turned down the invitation to.

My friend, Robyn was pleased to see me, if surprised, but there were so many people I didn't know there, and all I could do was smile at them. I also tried not to step on my friend's Chihuahua, which was getting under everyone's feet. I was looking for Robyn, as she had vanished in the crowd, but before I could find her a guy, that she'd once set me up on a date with, found me.

"Are you here with someone?" He winked at me, and I realised just how much bullshit he had spared me by not calling me back.

"We've met before."

Now it was his turn to look at me blankly. He couldn't remember. I couldn't believe it. While I wasn't too full about myself or my appearance, and knew I could be a piece of work when it came to guys, surely I was more memorable than this.

"Ah, of course we have." He winked at me again. He must've thought this was meant to be an attempt at flirtation. Oh, dear!

"I must have been mistaken. I am sorry." I was about to hurry away when he grabbed my arm.

"No, no. I think you're right. I'm awfully sorry; I'd remember such a pretty face." He smiled at me in a predatory way, and I realised no matter what he had thought about me before, what he saw now apparently passed as New Year's kiss material.

Oh, no. I didn't think so. It was amazing what a few glasses of bubbly could do to a human being.

"I really need to go now. It was nice to meet you." I tried to wrench my hand free.

"But you only just arrived."

He smiled wider, pulling me closer to him and I realised just how uncomfortable I was with this attention, his infringement of my personal boundaries. My friends had always said I should lighten up and I realised in this instant just how wrong they were. Relationships had always been serious for me. It was something I thought was worth working for. And hopefully good enough for someone to get past all these walls I had put up around myself. Whoever broke them down would deserve to see what's beneath. It didn't matter if it happened now, or in a decade. Why should I settle for anything less? Was I seen, as more desperate, just because I wasn't in a relationship? No-one had the right to think less of me because of something stupid like that. Not this guy, trying to get with the next best girl, not my 'supportive' friends and least of all myself. I realised that it wasn't me that needed to change but everyone around me - hell, even society.

As glad as I was about this epiphany, I still had this guy on my arm as if he was drowning and I was his bloody safety buoy. I had the feeling words wouldn't do too much to diffuse this situation. I looked past his face to the huge clock on the wall - it was just under a minute to twelve. He was practically pressing me against the wall. I saw no other way to get out of this, and I let myself fall onto my bum, not caring what this would do to either my dress or my dignity. Sadly, he didn't seem to care about those things either. He dropped down to my level, his lips inching closer and closer, with every tick of the clock. I twisted my head sideways, thinking that I only had to suffer this pawing another few seconds...

But why should I ever be forced to endure something, if I could change it? I saw my friend's Chihuahua scampering up to us, probably hoping we had some food. I grabbed the dog by the scruff of the neck, and swung it up in front of my face, just as Mr Lover had finally managed to cross that space.

The kiss must've felt different from what he was expecting. He looked startled, first at me, then at the dog. His mouth dropped open and he was picking Chihuahua fur out of his mouth. The dog looked startled at first, but soon its tail started wagging. Before I could find out if there was to be a happy ending in this star-crossed relationship, the world swam and I heard a motivating voice mutter 'Fast geschafft.' - *Nearly there.*

I woke again, not even noticing the vibrations in my hand anymore, not even bothering to check the clock. I flipped open my laptop and opened a document.

"Dear Colin, I would like to notify you of my resignation..."

Once I had started, I couldn't type the words quick enough. Before I knew it, I had the document printed and sealed into an envelope ready for a couple of days' time, when I would be back to work, ready to press it into my superior's hand. I bookmarked jobs at the companies whose sites I had swooned over, dreaming what it might be like working for them. I had still time to finish this, but there was something I had to do first.

I wore *the* dress, the one I had bought but had never dared to wear. The sequins had seemed to glare at me whenever I looked at it, making me think that I hadn't been ready to commit to wearing it, but now I was. The sequins still glowered, but I smiled as I whipped it over my body, putting some make up on and pinning my hair in a lazy, comfortable, top-knot. Of course, I remembered to accessorize too. I grabbed the bag with my beloved camera, which had been gathering dust, banished to the back of my wardrobe. I was lucky; there was still a little juice left in it. I slung it around my neck and grabbed my coat and shoes. I had somewhere I needed to be.

The city was overlooked by one of the world's wonders of construction, a bridge no one had thought possible before it was built. The bridge I had always wanted to visit, but never got around to, because life was too busy. It felt right that I would go there and greet the New Year, no matter what had happened before.

It was beautiful, even before the fireworks started. I could see my city; the city I had grown up in, in all its glory. In all this time, I'd never been here. I'd never seen all the windows illuminating the night, never seen it in its glorious entirety. Also, oddly enough, I felt a rush of anticipation at the thought of spending New Year's Eve with so many people I had never met before. Every single one of them had different hopes and dreams. Every single one was planning the New Year, whether they knew it or not. Not every one of them would succeed, but I could feel the potential and I blushed, remembering how I had wasted mine. I took pictures of the city and its luminous coat and the people that were with me being part of something bigger. No one minded the light drizzle that misted this part of the city.

It was a couple of minutes before twelve when I noticed a young man, by himself, an expression of awe on his face. He seemed so happy, so content. I wondered what his dreams were. He was sitting by one of the huge pieces that held the bridge suspended, his feet dangling off the structure. I could never be that daring, sequins aside. I didn't know if it was the breeze that had just come up or if something else was at play, but I felt drawn towards him. I heard my shoes clatter on the ground and before I had realised I was moving towards him.

He noticed me, smiled as he saw me approaching, one lone traveller recognising another.

"Hi." I said.

"Good evening." As he stretched over to shake my hand, I saw panic flash across his face, and I realised he must have slipped on the wet surface as he was moving to reach me.

I let go of my camera and grabbed his extended arm as hard as I could, dragging him over to my side of the bridge. He fell on me, scrambling quickly, as he realised where he had landed. I got up, picked up my camera and examined it for possible damage. But there was nothing; the lens had miraculously stayed on.

My nan used to wish me a good 'slide' into the New Year, just as she did earlier this evening in my dream. This, however, could have been anything but 'Guter Rutsch' for him, considering it was quite a drop.

"Wow! I mean thank you. I think you actually saved my life there..."

"That's okay, you're welcome."

He didn't say anything then, just stared at me and there was an odd silence in the air. I was about to turn to leave when he said:

"Do you think I could have your number? Just so I could invite you for a coffee?"

I smiled at him.

"Thank you," I said slowly.

As I walked away , with him still looking after me, I realised that maybe I didn't need saving at all. Since I was the one doing the saving. The clock hit twelve and I blinked. I was fully awake, walking away from the bridge with the firm determination to live up to my own hopes and dreams in the morning, not my friend's, my parents' or even my dear nan's. All I'd needed was a nudge in the right direction. This was my life and I firmly held the controller for it in my hand. I looked up to the fireworks exploding all around me and whispered "Guten Rutsch!" into the sky.

Last Sunday in October

The end of British Summertime

Ian Millsted

Jimmy kicked the back of the skateboard so that it flipped up and he could grab it. He tucked it under his arm. He knew it made too much noise to ride it any closer to number 87; the one his Mum's boyfriend called the prefab. The only one of the old single-storey houses that didn't get knocked down to make room for the new flats that got built. A funny little building surrounded by trees which were, in turn, surrounded by the four- and five-storey modern apartment blocks. Jimmy's Mum had said the owner had made a fuss about having their home bought by the council so that it could be knocked down. The building company, faced with negative stories in the local press, had relented, saying that as it was where they had planned to put in a pond they could leave it and just build around.

Jimmy didn't believe any of the stories about number 87 being haunted. He didn't believe in ghosts or anything that couldn't be seen.

"Okay, then," Ryan had said to him in front of the others "why don't you go and knock on the door?"

Ryan had then punched him in the privates, right in front of Kelly too, and had told him to 'man up'. What really freaked Jimmy out about number 87 was that the people there were supposed to be really old. Someone told him they'd been living there since the war. Was that even possible? Jimmy was twelve. His Mum was 31 and his gran was 50. He didn't really know any actual old people and those he saw in shops just seemed to get in the way and move too slowly.

Ryan and the others were back at the corner of the lane. He knew they would be watching him all the way. He tried to look casual as he walked along the little-used pavement. Half-way there, the tarmac path turned to mud; a message from the building company to the owners of number 87 that they were on their own, as they had asked to be. Tendrils from the overgrown hedge reached out to block his way. Jimmy kept going, trying not to use his arms to move the obstructions in case he drew extra attention to himself.

Number 87 itself was only partly visible from the path. Half the building, including the front door, was hidden by fir trees which had grown to three times the height of the building itself. As he got closer, Jimmy could now see that the way to the front door was obstructed by out-of-control blackberry bushes. There was, though, a path around the side which looked more used. Jimmy's Gran always used the back door of her house, never the front door. This must be the same. He allowed himself a glance back. A couple more steps and he would be out of sight of Ryan, Kelly and the others. He could just stand for a few minutes and then go back and tell them that he had knocked on the door.

One step, two, took him to the corner. From there he could see along the side of the building. It was quiet and the grass, still wet from the late October rain of the night before, showed recent footprints. He crept along tentatively. There was one window along that wall, frosted and above his head. It was slightly open. Jimmy held his breath as he continued. He'd just gone past when the sound of a toilet flushing broke the silence. He ducked, ludicrously, as if someone had thrown something at him. Rising up again he ran for the corner where, unable to hold it any longer, his breath burst from him. This was ridiculous. Why was he doing this? Who cared what Ryan said? Why should he bother whoever lived here? He turned to retrace his steps.

"Hello son."

In the shock of hearing a voice, Jimmy threw his hand out to grab hold of something to steady himself but succeeded only in knocking his fist against the house wall. He swore, then turned around and started apologising to whoever was there. “I’m sorry, you just scared me. I...”

“It’s usually my face that puts people off, not my voice.”

Jimmy stared at the man. He couldn’t help himself. He was old; properly old. He was standing on the back door step, looming over Jimmy. He wasn’t stooped like the pensioners in the shops but ramrod straight. His clothes looked all wrong for him, with long bony wrists protruding from frayed shirt sleeves. The shirt looked like it had once been smart, like Jimmy had to wear for school, but was all creased and had black smears down one side. It was worn over a blue vest or t-shirt and both were tucked into a pair of green trousers.

But it was the face that Jimmy kept coming back to, despite wanting to look at anything else. From the thinning hair on the old man’s head to the irregular whiskers on his chin ran a deep scar. It was an inch wide and indented far enough that Jimmy thought he could press his fingers deeper than the first knuckle joint. It cut through where one eye would once have been, leaving overlapping flaps of skin, and through the side of the nose where it twisted the flesh to give the impression of a permanent sneer, before stopping just below the mouth, but not before exposing the gums and yellowed teeth to full view.

“I’m sorry, mister. I’m just really sorry.” Jimmy turned and ran. He ran all the way to the corner where he discovered that Ryan and Kelly and the rest must have got bored and gone somewhere else. Only then did he realise he had pissed himself.

***

June peddled faster to catch up with Iris. The roads from Girton College to the railway station were quiet enough, with petrol rationing being policed firmly, that it was possible for the girls to hear each other talk as they rode along.

"I'm buggered if I'm going to let the boys beat us there," said Iris.

June laughed at the use of language and the cut glass pronunciation. Iris liked to use words of which her mother would not approve.

"They'll be taking full advantage of the Corpus breakfast before leaving," said June. "We've plenty of time."

The waiting room at Cambridge train station was occupied only by a mother with two young children and a group of three U.S. airmen carrying kit bags. Iris went off to buy tickets while June tightened the cords holding her bag on to the rack at the back of the bike.

"Look who I found by the ticket office," announced Iris on her return. A male student, Stefan, held the door open for her.

Stefan limped awkwardly as he followed Iris into the waiting room. "Bad news, I'm afraid. Rupert can't come. Some kind of summons back to the family; you know, some emergency at the Hall."

June glanced across at Iris and saw a brief, crestfallen expression before the brave face emerged triumphant.

"I'll understand if you want to cancel, or don't want me along," Stefan continued.

"Nonsense," said Iris. "The Ghost Society shall carry on resolutely. We have train tickets, food, wine and a real ghost story to explore."

***

Moira looked back down the road as she locked her car. She rarely saw anyone else near number 87 but still held a belief that it was one of the less safe areas she visited on her rounds. The district nurse badge she had seemed to be respected by most but nothing was guaranteed these days.

The trees had dropped enough pine needles and cones to make the path below her feet all but invisible. Her client had not been physically able to keep the gardens in order for some years now. Moira walked past the blackberry bush and down the side of the path. As she rang the back door bell she checked her bag again for the packet of loose tea.

Despite the shabby appearance of the house and gardens, this was still very much a loose tea and teapot household. The physical checks she had to do didn't really take all that long. Much of her job was really listening. At least the stories here were good; romantic liaisons in wartime London, all those characters at Cambridge University and that weird story about the boat.

The door opened inwards.

***

It was freezing. June sat at one of the two benches in the boat's small galley, huddled in two blankets over her clothes, including her winter coat which she had not quite got around to taking off. She had watched as Stefan had struggled earnestly with the Calor Gas connections for a couple of hours until finally he had got the stove working. Iris had left the grill on to provide heat while she cooked some sausages on the top ring. June wondered how Iris remained so indefatigably cheerful, despite the cold and the absence of Rupert.

The evening twilight was settling by the time Iris placed a large plate of sausages and fried tomatoes in the centre of the set-up table and invited June and Stefan to help themselves. This was soon joined by three glasses and a bottle of red which Iris handed to Stefan so he could 'do the honours'.

As the food warmed her inside, June started to relax. The day's journey had been tiring with three changes of train to reach Maldon and then a walk down to the river where they took possession of the canal boat. The three of them had worked out how to manoeuvre the boat quite quickly and they had travelled the six miles to Paper Mill Lock without incident. Even so, the afternoon was gone by the time they moored up and started to make things comfortable for the night.

As glasses were refilled, shadows from the gas lamps flickered on the curved internal walls. June looked at her friends. Iris was leaning back, with one foot curled underneath her and smoking her third cigarette of the evening. Stefan was sipping his wine; trying to make it last as long as possible.

"I think it's time," June said. "Who wants to go first?"

"I can," said Stefan. "I wrote something and showed it to Rupert."

Stefan started to read his story of an injured Great War veteran haunted by the ghosts of his former comrades. The girls knew that Stefan had been invalided out of the army after Dunkirk and had returned to Cambridge to continue his studies, an old man of twenty-two. Time failed to hide the autobiographical nature of the story, which was the closest to talking about his experiences that either June or Iris could remember from Stefan. As the story unfolded the protagonist started to live a double life wherein he existed normally in daylight hours but, during the nights, he found himself becoming a ghostly form. Stefan's voice started to crack a little as he read the final scene, in which the living ghost passes, intangibly and invisible, through a wall to observe, impotently, while his younger, able-bodied, brother proposes to the woman they both loved.

"So," said Iris when Stefan had gone to use the toilet, "was that me or you he was writing about?"

"He knows you're seeing Rupert and I have Archie," said June.

"I think it's you," Iris whispered.

June was saved from having to answer by the sound of the door opening. Iris raised a questioning eyebrow.

"Who's next?" said Stefan.

"I'll go," said June, keen to get things back under control. She started to read her own contribution; an attempt at a classical ghost story but with predominantly female characters. As she read it aloud for the first time she realised it was too cold, too clinical. Iris and Stefan listened politely.

***

It was just past two in the morning when June awoke to find the bed that had been occupied by Iris was empty. Despite the small size of the cabin, she'd not heard Iris get up. June slipped out of her sleeping bag and went to the door leading to the galley. She could hear voices, Stefan and Iris, from the other sleeping cabin at the other end of the boat. Whispered conversation and, well, she guessed Iris knew what she was doing. Was this trying to get back at Rupert for cancelling on her or did she just feel sorry for Stefan?

June sighed, picked up a packet of cigarettes and climbed up to the deck of the boat. She lit a cigarette, threw the match into the river and savoured the taste. Smoking, for June, was a solitary thing; something to be done while working on an essay in her room or on nights like this, when the clouds had got out of the way to reveal the stars. Was Archie up there somewhere, on his way back from another mission? His letters, when they came, never said much but she noticed that some of the names he had listed of friends he went to the pub with had not been mentioned for a while.

***

Archie was at the window watching through the net curtains as Moira drove away in her little car. She'd be back in two days, she'd said. Obviously things here were not bad enough yet to generate daily visits. He found her visits intrusive enough as it was.

"She means well," said June, reading and interrupting his thoughts.

"I know. I just prefer it when it is just the two of us. That was all I ever wanted; all I have ever wanted."

June paused and smiled across at Archie. He was still the man she had met and fallen for all those years ago. They had both been seventeen when they met, as people did back then, at a church social. She'd kept herself for him when he was conscripted and she'd gone off to Cambridge. He'd been tall and athletic and handsome then. Now he was old and she noticed that more than the disfigurement. His face had been scarred now for such a long time, she had got used to it, and saw beneath it, but his liver-spotted hands and need to pause after taking a few steps was more recent. Archie maintained that he still saw the same as he ever had, but she knew that wasn't true. She had certainly changed.

“I’m glad she reminded you to put the clock back tonight,” June said. “You’d never remember otherwise.”

“Of course I would.” *How could I forget that, of all things?*

***

“And here is the pond in which the beautiful Lady Alice Mildmay drowned, a tragic suicide resulting from the cruel treatment she received from her husband.” Iris was in her element. She was wearing a blue cloak over a flowing, full-length dress, both of which swirled about her as she acted out the story she was telling. June wondered how she had managed to fit the items into the not very large bag she had brought with her. They were friends despite their different personality types and it was these constant surprises that reminded June why she enjoyed her company.

The three of them had enjoyed a leisurely breakfast and then moved the boat a further mile until Iris had indicated a place to moor up again. She had then led them past some agricultural buildings until they reached the grounds of a large farmhouse by the name Great Graces.

“There used to be a manor house here,” Iris had told them as they walked past a stable. “Thirty or so rooms. All gone now, like the family that built it.” June was about to ask whether they ought to ask permission from someone to be there but Stefan pipped her to it.

“The people who farm it are sort of relatives,” Iris replied. “They are expecting us. All arranged ahead of time.” Iris had led them to the pond where she had started half-telling and half-performing the story of Sir Henry and Lady Alice Mildmay.

She took them down a wide pathway or walk until they reached a bridge over a small brook.

“Here,” she said, “is where Lady Alice is said to haunt us to this day. And it is here we shall return to tonight, to see if she will appear to us. We shall use our extra hour tonight for a bit of ghost hunting.”

It was cold again that night but nobody mentioned it as they duly made their way to the supposed site of Lady Alice’s nocturnal appearances. Stefan produced a hip flask from a hidden pocket of his overcoat and each of them drank in turn. Iris lit a cigarette.

"So," whispered Stefan, "is she supposed to haunt here as some kind of revenge on this Mildmay chap, or is she just trapped here?"

"Well if she turns up we can ask her, I suppose," Iris replied.

"It's as if she's suffering twice over," June said. "Once in life and again in death."

They sat in silence for some time after that. June noticed that Iris had slipped her hand into Stefan's but chose to act as if she were unaware of it. Eventually June struck a match in order to light a cigarette and saw by the glow that Iris and Stefan had fallen asleep leaning into each other. Before blowing the match out, she looked at her watch. It was one o'clock.

She got to her feet and walked away from the others in order to finish her cigarette. She stepped on to the bridge and stood at the mid-point, ready to toss the end in when she was done. As soon as she stood still she felt a shiver across her chest. Breathing suddenly became difficult. She grabbed the rail and gasped for breath; trying to pull some of the chill air through her teeth. As she did so her legs started to quiver beneath her.

As a sense of panic swamped her, June turned to get back to Iris and Stefan but her way was blocked by a shimmering outline of a young woman. The form was moving ever closer to her. The bridge was not big. June tried, in vain, to force her legs to move but they refused her command. The shape coalesced into a definite form, as clear as any human might be.

June saw how very young Alice Mildmay was. There was fear on the face in front of her. She felt an urge to enfold the ghostly figure within her arms; to hug her and show support. The ghost of Lady Alice reached a hand out. June held up her own hand to hold it. The moment she did so an icy pain shot right to her heart. She fell to the ground and all went black.

Minutes passed before June could raise even her head. By the time she did so, the ghost was gone. Her breathing steadied and she struck another match in order to look at her watch. Ten minutes until two o'clock in the morning.

The silence was broken by a low humming noise. June looked up. The sound grew louder. Too loud, too quickly. The hum turned to a whine and then to a deafening metallic scream.

***

Archie watched the boy running away from the house. He'd hoped the boy would stop long enough to talk a little. Archie wanted to ask him about skateboards and football and girls but he'd run off at first sight of his face; a constant reminder of the flight that didn't quite make it back to base that night in 1944. The reaction didn't surprise him. It was what always happened.

The day passed into evening. He sat quietly, watching his wife. She was beautiful to him.

They did as they did every year on this evening. The radio ran through the midnight news and the shipping forecast until Radio 4 gave way to the BBC World Service.

"The dark nights are coming," Archie said.

"There are always dark nights," June replied, "but the summer comes back again."

"I'm old, June. So old. I don't know if I'll see another summer."

Archie looked at the beautiful young woman in front of him. She hadn't aged a day. Why would she?

The radio announced that it was two o'clock British Summer Time and also one o'clock Greenwich Mean Time. Archie watched as June faded in front of his eyes. He was alone.

Burnton Cary

Roz Clarke

"You know how I feel about dead things!"

"Goodness, Fishy, you're such a squirmer. It's only a water rat or something. Come on, I want to take a closer look."

"You're horrible. And I *told* you, stop calling me that!"

Anne turned her back and folded her arms. She could hear her sister's footsteps ploshing ahead in the direction of the wet, furry body Lydia had spotted in the reeds. She screwed up her eyes against the sun, which set the water of the Levels coruscating every time it came out from behind the small clouds that swept overhead.

"It is a water rat, come and see," Lydia cried. "Find something to poke it with!"

"I don't want to poke it," said Anne, turning around despite herself. "Or see it." She looked anyway.

"Ooh, what's *that*," said Lydia, leaning down, her face so close to the water that the bow on the end of her plait trailed into it, yellow darkening to green.

"I'm not coming over there." But Anne's feet were taking her towards her sister, her ten-year-old's natural curiosity winning out over her squeamishness, something thrilling in her at the anticipation of whatever awful thing had Lydia so excited. Was the dead creature rotting, would its eyes have been pecked out, like the sheep they'd seen on the Brecons the summer before, picked only half-clean by carrion birds?

But Lydia's eyes were no longer on the dead vole at all; there was something dark under the surface of the water, a tangled shape pushing up from the bog. Lydia's foot slipped from the tussock she was perching on, and plunged into the morass below. She shrieked and scrambled back to firmer ground, but her face, as she called Anne over again, was flushed with delight. "I think there's a body here. Come on, hurry! A *dead* body."

Anne stopped again, a few feet away. Her hands clenched around her bunched-up skirt, which she still held high, though the battle to keep it dry had long been lost. "You mean *another* dead body. You already had one."

"No, silly fish, I mean a real body. A human one. I think I can see a hand. It's all brown and gnarled like an old stick but it's definitely got fingers. I can see fingernails, like terrible claws."

At that Anne's sense of dread dropped away, to be replaced by annoyance. "Can't you think of anything else to do besides try and frighten me? It's true, you aren't right in the head."

Lydia flicked her plait over her shoulder. "If you were less of a squirmer I wouldn't have to, would I?"

"It's not normal to be so obsessed with death. There's nothing wrong with me, it's you that's not right! Aunt Lettie said—"

"Aunt Lettie said, Aunt Lettie said! She's a mean old boot, and she's a hypocrite anyway. She was just mad because of her precious bird hat. And she wouldn't have said a word if her darling Alfred had done it. She hates me because I'm a girl. It's *so* unfair."

Anne couldn't see any sense in that. "I'm a girl too!"

Lydia rolled her eyes. "If you weren't such a goody-goody you'd understand."

Dismissing Anne, she crouched down over the water again, stirring the surface with her fingers, letting it slip over her wrist, until her forearm had disappeared. With a sudden cry, she slipped again, this time both feet going out from under her, and she toppled sideways into the bog. Anne lurched across the space between them, unable to find dry ground, the mud sucking at her feet. She reached down to Lydia, letting her skirts fall, her heart hammering in panic.

She'd heard stories about people who had walked out into the Levels and disappeared, about deep sink-holes invisible from the surface that could take you by the legs and pull you underneath the bog, as surely as a devil would pull you into hell.

Lydia accepted her help and struggled to her feet. One slimy hand was wrapped around Anne's freckled wrist, and the other grasped something Lydia had pulled up from the bog. It looked like a thick root. Anne felt a strong, sickening compulsion to look for fingernails; she twisted her head around so she couldn't see it. Lydia, balance restored, released her arm and brandished the thing triumphantly. Anne took the opportunity to take a step away.

"Where are you going, Fishy?"

Anne said nothing. She took another sucking step in the direction of the bank, towards the path that would take her back to the house. Aunt Lettie would be furious at the state of her dress. She swiped at the soggy fabric helplessly, and when she reached the spot where their shoes and stockings waited, patiently paired at the side of the path, she picked hers up and carried them, making her way barefoot between stones on one side and nettles on the other. She was trying not to cry at the thought of another five weeks at Burnton Cary with only Lydia, Aunt Lettie and Cousin Alfred for company.

When she saw two tousled blond heads above the scrub, coming round the curve of the path towards her, she ducked into the hedgerow, thinking she'd hide until they passed. She caught her naked ankle against a thick bramble, tripped and put both hands into a stand of stinging nettles. Alfred and Silas, their housekeeper's boy, didn't spot her where she crouched. They were deep in conversation, both smiling. She couldn't hear their words, but in her heart she felt sure they were talking about her, laughing at her. She yearned for home, and for her mother, but although nobody had said a word about it, she knew why she and Lydia had been sent away. The thought was so terrifying she had to turn her face away from it. She hugged her knees to her chest, and wept.

NINE YEARS LATER

The drawing room was the least unwelcoming room in the old house, once the dust sheets had been removed and the fire lit. Anne, Lydia, and the newest member of the Grange family, Alfred's wife Frances, had swept through the house making it as clean and homelike as possible before Alfred arrived from Bristol with Aunt Lettie. Colonel Grange, Anne and Lydia's father, had engaged the help of Silas, who had grown to be an affable, practical young man, and they had spent the afternoon checking over the grounds and ensuring that the horses would be safe and comfortable.

Anne had been looking forward to spending time with her father, but now that the four of them sat around the fire in the drawing room, which was still damp and chilly, an awkward silence had descended. Every time Colonel Grange went away on a campaign, Anne mused, she managed to forget the changes in their relationship that had come with the passing of time. It was no longer appropriate for her to throw her arms around his neck. She was uncomfortably aware of the need for proper decorum in front of Frances, who possessed finishing school elegance, and she hesitated to show her normal affection when her father seemed so very sombre and tired. Every so often he would glance around the room, a haunted look on his face, before sighing and returning his gaze to the sad little fire in the grate.

"Don't be too disappointed, Frances. We shall have a lively blaze tomorrow!" Anne said, her voice harsh after yet another too-long silence. "Alfred will enjoy chopping the logs."

Lydia stirred in her chair, as if shaking off some discomfort. She had clearly been going to say something, but caught Frances looking at her and held her tongue.

"We shall have to set him chopping for certain," said Frances brightly. "He has promised me a great fire for Bonfire Night, since we shall miss the festivities in Clifton. They have quite a thrilling show, with fireworks and a Guy Fawkes paraded through the streets before they burn him on the pyre. Shall we have our own Guy Fawkes, do you think?"

"If you would like to make one, Frances," said Lydia, "feel free to rummage around. This house has a great many mouldy old trunks and wardrobes, but no hidden treasures or family skeletons. If you like moths and spiders you're in for a treat."

Anne spotted her father flinching at the mention of family skeletons. It mirrored her own feelings. A cold knot of dread and fury bit at her stomach several seconds before she worked out what it was that had brought it on in her. She twitched violently, and covered it by hastily standing. "I'll fetch the bed-pans and warm them on the fire. The bedrooms are going to be icy tonight."

She left the room as casually as she could manage, grateful that there wasn't more light. She forced herself to breathe deeply. On the stairs, safely out of sight, she leaned against the wall and inhaled the musty smell of a house left empty for too long. Throwing open the windows that afternoon had done nothing but let the damp air in. It was the second of November, and an especially long, wet autumn was giving way to an early winter; snow had already fallen twice. Black mould had crept onto the wallpaper beneath the stairs window and in the corners of the bedrooms in the older of the two wings. The roof needed mending, and Alfred would decide during this trip whether to refurbish the old place and live in it, or try to sell it. That would come down to whether Frances liked it or not. The alternative was to share the town house in Bristol with Aunt Lettie. Anne shuddered. Poor Frances was caught between Scylla and Charybdis, and for herself, Anne did not want either future to unfurl. She had liked it best when the house was shut up, abandoned, forgotten.

The door to the box room creaked, just as it had done when they were children. Anne held her breath as she opened it, as if that could make a difference. They had not looked into this room during their whirlwind of airing and dusting, but Frances was bound to come in here sooner or later; if not in her quest for Guy Fawkes rags, then in her beady-eyed assessment of her possible future home.

Anne opened the built-in cupboard in the farthest corner, hauled out a pile of moth-eaten red blankets, and felt for the loose board at the side by the chimney stack. Where the chimney sloped inwards, the side of the cupboard was straight, leaving a small space behind. Anne had discovered it, and kept it a secret. Knowing something about Burton Cary that the others didn't had helped her survive.

She drew forth a dusty cloth-wrapped bundle, which she draped in one of the red blankets and carried into the room that was to be hers for the week. Lydia had claimed the room they'd shared as girls, and Anne was glad. She had some good memories of that room, from when her mother had been alive and had sung them to sleep on drowsy summer evenings, but these were overlaid by the later memories, of waking screaming in the night, Lydia comforting her as though the darkness unlocked some well of sisterly sympathy, only to scare her again the next night with her tales of ghosts and creeping things. And worse. Anne shoved the bundle under her eiderdown, almost chuckling at the irony, though her hands trembled. She pulled the warming pan out from under the bed. This time, she would summon the strength to get rid of the thing before they returned to Gloucester.

***

Aunt Lettie's playing on the pianoforte was still confident and fluid, but her voice was no longer either. Her repertoire was extensive, and this performance had been going on since just after supper.

"Why don't you sing something for us, Frances?" asked Lydia. Anne hissed under her breath. She knew that sweet tone too well.

"Oh I couldn't," said Frances. "I would love to, some other time, but I'm afraid my throat is quite sore. All the dust, perhaps."

Lettie smiled. "We shall look forward to it, my dear. I'm sure you must have a quite lovely singing voice. Alfred could hardly help but have a discerning ear."

Frances looked at Alfred, but the young man was busy shuffling the stack of scores on top of the piano. Poor Frances. It would do her no good if she *could* sing; Lettie would not gladly suffer a rival in that department.

Perhaps it wasn't diplomacy, though. Anne's own throat, she realised, was also sore. Lettie had brought her lady's maid, Martha, and with two extra pairs of hands they had turned the house inside out and upside down before putting it back together again, smelling sweeter and cleaner than Anne remembered it ever smelling.

Luck had brought them clear weather, and though it was even colder than before, it was a good, crisp cold that invigorated the lungs, rather than the seeping, spore-laden damp of previous weeks. However, the dust that they'd beaten out of rugs and curtains and swept from damp-despoiled rows of books had had them all coughing up black sputum by the end of the day.

Alfred, true to expectation, had chopped enough logs for a proper fire, and piled the fallen branches and rotten wood from the woodland at the edge of the pasture and the dark river banks into an enormous mound on what had been the back lawn, before it had been abandoned to brambles, nettles and wildlife. He and Silas had started to clear the brambles. It would be a fine blaze indeed, if the weather held dry until Wednesday.

"Why don't you tell us all about your trip to Africa, Lydia?" Alfred asked, putting the scores down with the flourish of a man whose brainwave has brought him great relief. "You must have had some fascinating adventures."

Lettie pushed back the piano stool, pursing her lips. "Africa, indeed. It's a wonder she hasn't come back with some dreadful disease. I do hope you've had your fill of uncivilised places, Lydia, and will take my advice and settle down before you *do* catch something disgusting. You are older than Alfred here. We must even start thinking seriously about a match for Anne. It's not going to be easy, with Lydia so wilful and Anne so mousy and plain."

Aunt Lettie sat on the settee next to her brother-in-law and put one hand on his arm. "Do speak to them, Nathanial! These poor girls have nobody but me to help them find suitable matches, but Lydia has never listened to anything her poor aunt says. *You* must persuade her."

Colonel Grange patted her gloved hand and nodded. "Damascus is not as uncivilised as you might think, my dear. I am quite sure Dr and Mrs. Beaumont took excellent care of our Lydia. Sylvia entrusted Mrs Beaumont with the girls' care several times when she was alive – our trust in her was second only to our trust in you and William."

Aunt Lettie was not mollified by this. She sniffed, which brought on a sneeze. Lydia stifled a giggle in her own handkerchief.

Col Grange continued: "Why don't you let Lydia tell you all about it, and you may judge for yourself. Lydia?"

Anne picked up her needlework. She and her father had already heard Lydia's stories. If they hadn't, Col Grange would never have risked this move. Anne could only hope Lydia would not betray his trust by telling the kind of story she really relished; the kind that brought you suddenly awake in the darkest hours of night with your heart beating fit to burst and your ears ringing with terror.

She was almost disappointed when Lydia concentrated on safe subjects such as food and history, and left out all but the most innocuous information about the dig and the things they had found. Anne knew about these because Lydia had written her letters, which she had promised to keep, to supplement the diary and notes Lydia had kept during her trip. Her sister, far from planning to settle down, was hoping to write a book about ancient death rites and customs.

Anne, on the other hand, rather envied the young Mrs Alfred. Not that she would have wanted her cousin for a husband, heaven forbid. He was less of a mummy's boy than he had been, but too much one for her to bear. And Aunt Lettie was bad enough as an aunt; the thought of her as a mother in law... She shuddered, then smiled to be shuddering over such a mundane thing. It was pleasant to be distracted from the darker thoughts that crept into her anxious mind.

***

"That'll be a job to light," said Silas morosely, nudging a piece of sodden wood at the edge of the bonfire with his boot.

"It's been dry all day." Alfred protested.

"Then best 'ope it's dry all day tomorrow an' all. Peat's not dry enough to catch without the fire's hot. Never knowed such a mis'rable year. You 'member 'ow to cut kindlin' down?"

"I haven't forgotten. But a little practice never goes amiss, eh? Let's light a little fire now and see how we go on."

Anne was standing back a little from where Alfred and Silas were cutting kindling, to get to the dry hearts of the slimy logs, and rekindling their friendship into the bargain. Despite their differing backgrounds, the two were alike in many ways. Hunched over the wood, knives in their hands stripping bark, and muffled in their coats and scarves, you could barely tell them apart. She didn't know if they'd kept in touch during the years the house had been shut up, but since the end of that summer, they'd had even more in common: both had lost their fathers.

Anne had spent long weeks dreading the news of her mother's death, while the boys ignored her and Lydia dealt with the fear in her own special way. Yet before the leaves had turned brown, Alfred's father had died and Silas's father run away with a girl from Yorkshire, whilst Sylvia had lingered on until almost Christmas. All of them half-orphaned, but it hadn't brought Lydia, Anne and Alfred any closer together.

She sidled over to the wood pile. It had a kind of beauty; the same air of grand dilapidation that the house was starting to develop. Fallen branches were tangled together in a mass of birch bark like rotted white brocade, decorated with dusty green lichens and the gentle frills of multi-coloured fungi. It would be a fine enough end to the house, if Frances didn't want it. What would be left? A few unrecognisable lumps of metal where the candlesticks had fallen? Or would more of the place, of their time there, be preserved in the peat? She hoped not. She liked the idea of Burnton Cary softly, prettily rotting and returning to the marsh.

Her train of thought was interrupted when she caught sight of a queer looking slug, creeping over one of the peat blocks that were stacked within the branches. It was paler than any slug she had seen before, a pinky-grey that was only a shade or two off white, and translucent at its edges. She leaned in to get a closer look. It had a delicate, if unsettling, beauty. She thought of the flames licking around it, cooking it alive, but she wasn't sure she could bring herself to touch it, to save it. Now that she was looking properly, she could see more of them, smaller, crawling over the soft wood and the dark peat. There was another... and another; they were everywhere. The whole pile was alive with them. A tremor of disgust ran from her scalp to her tail bone, and she turned and retreated to the house.

She found Frances, as she'd thought she would, sitting on the floor in the middle of the box room, surrounded by open trunks and boxes. She had started to assemble a figure from discarded clothing. Anne helped her finish it. They were packing everything away again when Lydia came into the room.

"Ah, the villain Fawkes himself, the very image."

Frances beamed at her. "Anne made the beard from a bit of an old moth-eaten fur stole. Isn't it wonderful and hairy?"

"Wonderful," Lydia echoed. "He needs a hat, though."

"I only found one hat," said Frances. She reached up to the top of a stack of boxes and pulled down a faded hatbox. Inside was Aunt Lettie's bird hat. On a nest of black, iridescent feathers, two yellow finches were posed as if about to take off, their little wings outstretched. They bobbed when Frances picked the hat up, trembling on a pair of springs. One of the birds' wings was broken, and flapped at an awful angle. Lydia let out a snort of unladylike laughter.

"Oh my gracious, that dreadful thing. How perfectly perfect. Put it on him. Let's see."

"Aunt Lettie will have a fit," said Anne.

"It's been mouldering here forgotten for nine years."

"Since you used it for target practice. She won't have forgotten that."

"Aunt Lettie doesn't need to know," said Lydia, and she winked at Frances.

***

"Roll on tomorrow, eh Frances?" said Lydia, taking her bowl of kedgeree to the window and standing there with it, careless of the rice grains that fell from her fork. "Another day in this place I think I can just about bear, as long as the rain holds off. You've no idea how ghastly it is when it's wet. Mud on everything."

"I didn't imagine you'd mind the dirt," Frances replied from her seat at the breakfast table. "What with all the digging and so forth."

"Grubbing about in holes," Alfred put in with a smirk. Lydia scowled at him.

"We're uncovering important historical facts. You can learn a great deal from the things people leave behind."

"Have you really dug up dead people?" asked Frances. "Wouldn't that be *horrid*?"

Alfred swallowed a bite of toast, frowning at Frances's eager expression. "Rather disrespectful, I'd say, though I suppose they are all heathens out there. It's not as though you're disturbing a proper Christian burial."

"Actually there are a good number of Christians in Syria, Alfred, which you'd be aware of if you'd ever taken an interest in the world beyond these turgid shores." She waved her fork at the dreary vista outside the window, scattering rice in all directions. "And no, Frances, it isn't horrid at all."

She thought for a moment before continuing. "Once someone's dead, they aren't a person any more. Whatever it was that made them a person – their soul, if you like – is no longer there. We treat them with respect, of course, Dr Beaumont isn't a tomb robber. But when you touch the skin of someone who died hundreds or thousands of years ago, it's just like leather. Even if it's clear they died in some dreadful way, it's very... remote."

"I sometimes wonder if we're sisters at all," said Anne, with a brittle laugh. She felt sick inside. Sleep had been a long time coming, and she'd woken early, and at both ends of the night, her head and heart had been filled with visions of decay, and stirred by deep, unexamined grief.

"You don't agree?" asked Frances.

Anne shook her aching head. There was a light in Lydia's eyes, a dangerous, familiar light. Anne looked down at her cold toast, willing Fate to unwind and take back what she'd just said, but it was too late.

"Anne's imagination is stronger than her intellect, Frances. No great flaw in a *lady*. It's perfectly fashionable, isn't it, to believe in spirits that speak to one after death? To think we're all surrounded by the restless dead, just waiting for a chance to push their long, rotting fingers through the veil and claw at our-"

"I never thought—" Anne started, but Alfred was speaking over both of them.

"Absolute nonsense, Lydia. Anne has never believed in such tosh, and you don't either, do you darling?"

Frances smiled and dipped her chin in agreement.

"We could prove it to them, couldn't we, Fishy? We could go back and find it... You could show everyone how *much* you don't believe in ghosts and ghouls."

"Find what?" asked Frances and Alfred together.

"Bog body," said Lydia casually, just as though it hadn't been her and Anne's darkest secret since they were children. Anne's skin froze, then crawled, then burned.

"You'd never..." she whispered.

"Never what? Find it? I'm sure I could. I don't know why I didn't think of it before. If I do it properly- I could write it up. I could take it to the British Museum. It could make my name." She put her bowl down and took Frances's hand in hers. "Will you help me look?"

Frances might have done, but Alfred forbade it. He tried to forbid Lydia too, but with Col Grange not answering to knocks at the study door, Lydia answered to nobody. She donned sturdy boots and a fur coat and hat, and strode away down the path, shovel in hand.

A voice came from behind Anne and Frances, who were watching her from the lounge window. "I found my old hat in the kitchen next to that vile effigy, you foolish girls- Where's Lydia going?"

"Oh, Lady Grange. Are you feeling better?"

"Not really."

"Lydia's going to do some archaeology in the bog."

Lettie sniffed thickly. "Rubbish. There's no archaeology in Burnton Cary."

"Oh but there is," said Frances, sparkling with innocent charm. "When Lydia and Alfred – and Anne – were children, Lydia found a bog body. That's a body that's been preserved in the peat, so that even after hundreds and hundreds of years, you can still see the person's face, and clothes – everything's still there. I would have thought dead people would rot right away, in all that mud, but apparently they don't. It's called *mummification.* And Lydia's writing a book about ancient people based on what they've found out from looking at *mummified* bodies, and all this time there's been one right here, only she hadn't thought to go and get it. Until now."

Frances's gaze had returned to the icy path as it wove, mottled white and brown, between the hedgerows to appear farther down, atop the bank that emerged from the bog as the fields dropped away. So she didn't see what Anne saw: Lady Letitia Grange ashen-faced and trembling, the composure, which had heretofore been total, in all of Anne's experience, briefly but thoroughly lost. And as swiftly regained.

"Alf*red*! Nathani*al*!"

The two men nearly collided in the doorway. Lettie's shriek had been fit to summon the dead. She pointed out of the window, stabbing the air with one taloned finger, her other hand curling so tightly around the bird hat that iridescent feathers were crushed and broken.

"Go and get that... that-" she choked, unable to utter words condemning enough. "That *girl*! She wants to – oh I have never been so *mortified* in all my life."

"I spoke to her, Mother, but Lydia was set on it. There's no chance she'll find it, so—"

"You *knew*?" Her hand whipped around and slapped Alfred soundly across the cheek. He fell back, holding his hand to his face in disbelief. "And you, Nathanial, have you given this revolting plan your blessing? I told you to discipline that child. You've been soft on them ever since Sylvia took ill."

"She's gone to dig up ancient remains," Frances chipped in, helpfully.

The cloud that had darkened Col Grange's features threatened to erupt into a storm of rage. Heedless of the effort it was taking him to hold back, Lettie continued: "You must go and bring her back at once. I won't have that hoyden dragging the family name through the mud with her heathen ways."

Anne watched, transfixed, as her aunt and her father locked eyes. Col Grange was livid. Was he angry with Lydia? He didn't say anything, but it seemed he was mostly angry with Lettie. Anne knew what she would have said in his place: that the family name was only hers by marriage, that Lettie knew nothing about raising girls, that she was a mean-spirited old besom who sucked all the joy out of life and wasn't fit to even breathe her mother's name – but there was a depth to her father's fury that went well beyond such petty matters, beyond anything she'd seen in him before. Still he said nothing.

Lettie finally looked at him and saw what was roiling beneath the surface. She knew. Whatever it was, Lettie understood it, and it came as a shock. The pallor returned to her skin, and her knees sagged. It was Anne who leapt to Lettie's side and caught her, preventing her from crumpling to the floor. Alfred moved to take his mother's other arm, and they settled her in one of the high-backed chairs. Col Grange spun on his heel and left the room.

"Has he gone to look for her?" Frances asked.

"I don't know," Anne answered. "I'm not altogether sure what just happened."

Lettie appeared to be in a dead faint, but Anne could see tears collecting in the wrinkles at the corners of her eyes.

"I'll go and find Lydia," said Alfred. "I'll get Silas to help."

Lettie's arm shot out from the enclosing chair and caught his wrist. Her eyes snapped open, pinning him with their intensity. "Not Silas."

"He knows the marsh better than anyone."

"Not Silas," Lettie repeated. "He mustn't-" She coughed. "Nobody must know what that girl is doing. We could never look the locals in the eye again." That undercurrent, whatever had passed between Lettie and Col. Grange, was still there. It seemed to Anne that the hand clutched tightly around Alfred's wrist was no longer a predatory claw, but the pale hand of a drowning woman, holding on for dear life.

***

Anne went with Alfred in the end, as only she knew where the girls had found the bog body, all those years before. They met Lydia on the path, coming back towards the house, shovel held jauntily over her shoulder. She waved to them.

"It's gone," she called. "Or I've misremembered the spot. They've cut the peat from that whole section." She waved her arm, taking in a swathe of marshland to the west. "It all looks very different. But I went carefully, and I couldn't find any trace."

Alfred sighed relief. "I didn't think you'd find it. It's a shame about your book. But Mother might have turned her toes up if you'd brought it back to the house. She doesn't think the dead should be disturbed."

"Not to worry," said Lydia, fixing Anne with a meaningful look. "*All* might not be lost."

***

What did you do with it, Fishy? the note read. Anne supposed she was grateful Lydia hadn't just upped and asked her in front of everyone over lunch. She folded the note and pushed it into the depths of the bonfire, taking care not to touch any of the slugs that still decorated the slimy wood and peat. The stack had not dried, despite another crisp, fine day. It looked, if anything, wetter than the day before. Tomorrow night, they would light it, come what may. Alfred had readied a drum of lamp-oil, should all Silas's skill at firelighting not prove sufficient.

Under the cover of writing a shopping list for Martha, Anne had written her response. *I have told you already. You will not find it.* She'd put her note in Lydia's pocket, and slipped up to her room. She should have buried the hand when she'd first claimed it. A month of finding it in her bed, or in her trunk, and Lydia giggling hysterically while Anne fled the room in tears and hid in the box room so that nobody would see her weeping... Every time, she had come back to find the hand removed, ready for Lydia to play the same trick again.

A month at least, and Anne had finally realised that the only way to stop Lydia was to deprive her of her vile relic. She would not have put it past her sister to smuggle the thing back to the house in Gloucester and continue tormenting her indefinitely. So the next time Lydia was otherwise engaged, she'd searched her sister's things until she'd found it, thrown the cloth over it so she could pick it up without touching it, and stashed it in the box room. Lydia was the smart one, but she was not as good at secrets as Anne.

She'd expected a furious response, but Lydia had, on finding it gone, turned to her with wide eyes and said "Maybe you're not such a squirmer after all!" She hadn't stopped trying to upset Anne with ghost stories, not until their mother passed on, but the nightly torture came to an end.

With the bonfire hiding her from the house, Anne untied the ribbon from the bundle. It was summer-sky blue, had hardly faded. The cloth was a cotton pillow-slip, stolen from the linen cupboard, now stained grey-brown by the dust. She turned back a corner, and revealed two finger-tips, with nails thick and cracked. She pulled the remaining folds aside. The hand was large, and brown like tea-stains, or tree roots. She touched it, and found Lydia had spoken truly; it didn't feel like skin. It was too hard, too cold.

But to Anne, it didn't seem inhuman. She knew this hand had once been attached to a living, breathing person. It had held food, tools, the hands of loved ones. Through it, someone had experienced life, and death. She wondered if the chill mud of the swamp was the last thing they'd felt, or if they'd died elsewhere. The kinds of questions Lydia and her colleagues might be able to answer, but they wouldn't do it right. Anne gently touched her fingertips to the dead man's fingertips and shuddered. A long breath escaped her lungs; almost a sigh, almost a sob. She wrapped the hand again, then thrust the bundle into the black shadows at the heart of the pyre.

Across the Levels, dusk was already gathering, and all that seemed to stir was the cool mist that clung to the rushes and caressed the lightless water.

***

"Are you well, Mother?" asked Alfred, hastening to her side. A moment earlier Lettie had been playing a melancholy tune. Then her hands had faltered, and when she lifted them from the keys, they shook. Lettie steadied herself on Alfred's arm, but she didn't look at him. Her gaze was fixed on the window, where Frances and Lydia stood holding the drapes back. They were discussing the prospect of rain falling in the night. From where Anne was sitting she could not see the sky, only the reflection of the lamplight.

Lettie struggled to her feet. She gestured towards the window, and Alfred helped her take a step forward. "Someone," she gasped. "...outside. He looked right at me."

"There's nobody there," said Frances. "Was it Silas?"

Col Grange snorted. "Why would Silas be peering in at us from the garden? He has the key to the kitchen door. Your mother-in-law is suffering from nervous exhaustion. There *is* nobody there and there *was* nobody there."

Anne stepped up to Frances and pulled back the curtain she had let fall. There was no moon, and she could see nothing but vague shapes in the darkness; black on black.

But when she glanced down, she noticed, at waist height on the glass, five shining trails of slime, as if five snails or slugs had ascended the window in formation. There were no snails or slugs at the ends of the silvery paths. Perhaps, she thought, the trails had fooled Lettie into seeing a face where no face was. But the tingling cold at the back of her neck and the leaping, irregular thrum in her chest suggested otherwise.

***

La Luna had shrugged off her shroud and a sliver of light lay across Anne's woven rug, pointing at the bedroom door. She had no memory of a dream, but a sense that she'd been running, or trying to, from someone she had betrayed, someone to whom her life was owed.

Over the rush of her blood in her ears, she could hear someone speaking, in a low, insistent tone. She pushed her feet out from the warm nest of her bed, and almost changed her mind. It was cold enough to see your breath. She pushed her toes into her waiting slippers, and crept to the door. It creaked loudly as she edged it open, but the flow of words continued, uninterrupted. Lettie's bedroom door, opposite, was open, and the room was flooded with moonlight. Anne strained to hear the person engaged in conversation with her aunt, but only Lettie's voice emerged.

Mouse-quiet, she padded across the hallway and put her head around the door. Lettie was standing with her back to Anne, facing the window. The curtains were drawn back. On the other side of the glass, an insubstantial shape appeared to hover, or... no, it was *clinging* to the window. It was big; taller than Lettie; it filled the space. Its outline was smooth, rippling, and the moonlight shone through it. Its centre was darker, and contained the impression of a human form. The more directly she looked at it, the hazier it seemed, but when she looked only with the corner of her eye it seemed quite real. Sidelong, she tried to make out its features, tried to read the shape of its limbs.

Naturally Anne was afraid; indeed, she was so afraid that her throat started to close and her knees threatened to give beneath her. She stood frozen to the spot, feeling as if she could liquefy entirely at any moment, seep into the faded carpet and disappear. But Anne was *good* at being afraid. Anne had spent all her life being afraid of such things as this, and so it didn't come as a shock to her, as it might have to someone more rational in outlook. She ignored her body's responses, and concentrated on listening.

"Why now? When he's so happy, why..." Lettie's voice was ragged, her words broken. "I looked for you. The nightmares... I couldn't bear the thought of you out there alone. I was so lost without William, and I couldn't stay. Once I'd gone, I couldn't bear to come back. I was a coward, I admit that, but no, I'm not sorry! Poor Silas, poor Maud... But there was nothing I could have done. You must understand. I had every right."

Gradually, strength was returning to Anne's muscles, but she couldn't make herself move into the room, or call out to her aunt. The thought of interrupting this dreadful, one-sided conversation was impossible. She wanted to go back to bed, but she was too afraid. She drifted backwards, barely aware of her own motion. Without deciding to, she did what she'd always done in case of night terrors, whenever the choice was there. She scampered silently, lightly, quick but not *too* quick, to her father's room.

"Father?" It felt transgressive to open the door, much less cross the threshold. Luckily he woke at once and got out of bed, with a soldier's instant alertness. "It's Aunt Lettie."

The colonel pulled his dressing gown on over his flannel pyjamas and followed Anne back to Lettie's room. Lettie was sitting on the edge of the bed, the bedspread bunched up in her lap, her hands worrying at it. She gazed unseeingly into the shadows, but her lips were still moving. Of the ghastly thing at the window there was no sign. Anne opened the window to make sure, letting a blast of cold air in. The exterior of the window was covered in one enormous slime trail; clear, thin, but definitely not a figment of her imagination. Something *had* been there.

"I won't compound my guilt with another lie," Lettie said suddenly and loudly. "I can't say I didn't mean to do it. I meant to. I just wasn't certain that I had." She raised her face to the colonel's. "Will you disown me now, Nathanial, and claim your inheritance? At least I won't hang, no, he'll come for me first. But Alfred... my poor child... It was all for him..." Here, she began to wail, a soft keening lament. She curled forward, grabbing for breath, then she arched backwards and her arms flailed wildly.

Anne's father sat beside her and gathered her to him, which surprised Anne almost more than anything else had that night. "Hang, Lettie?" he said softly. "What did you do?"

"You know, you *know*," she sobbed. "All these years I thought nobody knew, but all along *you knew*."

"No more of this now, Lettie. Anne, please wake Martha and ask her to bring her mistress a cup of hot milk and sit with her, then you must return to bed. I'll be in the study."

He released Lettie and ushered Anne out of the room ahead of him.

***

Lettie did not come down the next morning. Martha took her a tray, and brought it back untouched. Alfred wanted to send for a doctor, but Col Grange assured him that Lettie would be better left to recover; it was only nerves, nothing medical. True enough, but her father hadn't seen what Anne had.

Her chance to speak to her father alone came when the others went outside to watch Silas lighting the bonfire.

"Before I came to wake you, Father, Lettie-" She faltered, unable to speak of the strange apparition. "Lettie said some things. Forgive me for asking but I must. What did she do? I know it has something to do with Silas."

"You should not ask, Anne. Let it be."

"Are Silas and Alfred brothers? Did Uncle William-"

"Your uncle did nothing."

"She said you know.? She said 'poor Silas's and 'poor Maud'. I take it Maud is Mrs. Dale? What happened?

Lettie can't have had anything to do with Silas's father disappearing, surely?"

"Anne! Hold your tongue. You appear to have forgotten your manners. That's not like you at all."

He looked at her sternly. She knew she must look a sight; she hadn't slept all night and had spent the day avoiding everyone by walking in the marsh, despite the rain that had returned to the Levels in full and bitter force.

The Colonel's expression softened. "It was Lettie's maid that Samuel - Silas's father - went off with. I know she feels responsible."

"No. There was more to it than that. You wouldn't disown her for that. She wouldn't *hang* for that. And who is it that's going to come for her?"

"She's having some sort of nervous episode. Delayed grief, in my opinion, triggered by returning to Burnton Cary. The last day she, and I, were here was the day of William's funeral." He frowned. "Perhaps she is entertaining some mad notion that Samuel will return from Yorkshire, or wherever the reprobate went off to."

"Why would she fear that?"

"No more questions, Anne."

So. The angry shadows swirling in the undercurrent were *secrets*. Dark secrets. Dangerous secrets. Anne saw them disturb her father's features before his face closed over them again, and she was dismissed.

Walking in the ruined garden, Anne puzzled it over. What she understood, though only opaquely, of what Lettie might have done, seemed to fit together neatly enough, but there was something awry. She kept finding her fingertips rubbing against one another of their own accord, and the sensation of cold, old skin reached into her mind, stroking chill, slippery fear into her soul.

Old skin. Ancient fear. *Ancient* betrayal. Anne knew, on a level deeper than consciousness, that *she* had summoned this thing. She had reached across the years, beyond the veil, and brought it out of exile. So why was it focussed on her aunt? In the chaos of her mind, pieces of the puzzle snagged against one another, and some of them caught, until finally understanding came.

Silas's father hadn't run away, or at least Lettie didn't believe so. She thought the body Lydia had found was his. Anne's fingertips tingled with the memory of the dead hand's touch. Lettie thought this ghoul was Samuel, and she must have good reason to think so. And the manifestation was drawn to her guilt like moths to candles. Anne glanced over her shoulder at the bonfire. She knew, as surely as she knew this was her doing, that the spirit menacing her aunt was old, unimaginably old. She should say something. She should get the hand from the stacked fire and give it to Lydia, who could prove it. Lettie might be guilty, but nobody had to know. The family could keep its secrets. But how would the spectre be laid to rest? Would it turn in her direction?

Anne drew her thoughts inside her, and took the path down to the bog.

***

She'd barely closed the kitchen door behind her when the scream rang out. She opened it again and tumbled back outside. Lydia, Alfred, Frances and Silas, who had been busy at the bonfire, came pell-mell across the muddy lawn, Silas brandishing a lit torch. The rain had stopped but the air was still thick with moisture, and the bonfire barely smouldered behind them. The wind eddied and the tang of smoke reached Anne. As the scream faded, the sound of splintering wood and broken glass followed it.

"You won't show them anything! I won't let you destroy my family!"

They ran along the side of the house, and gathered beneath Lettie's window. Or rather, the gaping hole where her window had been. Broken glass and half-rotten wood lay scattered on the ground. Silhouetted against the light within the room, Lettie stood, brandishing a cast-iron candlestick. Her outline was blurred, and seemed to shift. Anne blinked. *It was there*. Bigger than the night before, or perhaps she could just see more of it. She looked at the faces around her.

"Do you see it?"

"Mother!" Alfred shouted. Lettie didn't seem to hear him.

So... close, a voice whispered in Anne's ear. She started, turned to see... nothing. *Guilty...* it said.

Eyeless but alive I was buried and breathed naught but mire, but the worms did not feed on me. I fed on them, their tiny souls sustained me for so... long in the darkness. Alone. Lost. I will show them where. I will have my vengeance. Yours is the guilt.

There were words, but there were no words. A voice, but no voice spoke.

"Leave us alone!" screamed Lettie.

Anne's stomach turned over. It was clear that the others neither saw nor heard what was all too clear to herself and her aunt.

"You want an eye for an eye," said Lettie. "You'll have it. But you won't pull my family apart."

And she thrust her candlestick deep into the dark centre of the spectre, her full weight behind it. To everyone else, it would have seemed that Lettie threw herself bodily from the window in a fit of madness. Only Anne could see the rippling boundary of the ghastly form wrapping close around Lettie, pulling her down with it.

When they hit the ground, the crunch of breaking bones was cushioned in the squelching of soft, moist flesh. Lettie lay face down in the grass, unmoving. Anne flinched, automatically looking away. That gave the thing solidity. The blurred darkness sharpened into a human form; a man; young and beautiful, ancient and hideous all at once. Black pits of eyes glared straight at Anne, and brown arms, suntanned and muscular, mud-brown and withered, reached out to her.

I will show you where. I will drag you into darkness.

Behind the fury was a terrible void of loneliness, a thousand nights without stars. Anne closed her eyes. It was all too easy to understand. *I'm sorry,* she thought. *You aren't alone.* She opened her eyes again, stared back at the dead man, and saw nothing but her own tears.

She wiped her sleeve across her face, leaving it wet with gathered mist, and misery. Unwatched, the bonfire had seethed into life behind them. Stuttering in orange light and black shadow, Lettie's crumpled body looked very small. Beneath the body, and the pool of blood that flowed gently from it, the glimmering translucence of the ancient wraith melted into the earth. In Anne's mind's eye, delicate, moist white slug bodies shrivelled to nothing in the cruel flames.

***

"I always suspected they were brothers," said Lydia. "But I assumed it was an indiscretion on Uncle William's part. I am rather sorry that I thought it of him, when he was the innocent party."

"William evidently knew Samuel was Alfred's father. He paid a stipend to the family from Alfred's birth until he died. I found the details when William's accounts were passed to me in trust for Alfred. At first I assumed the same as you did, Lydia, that William had begotten Silas. But in amongst his papers was a letter from a Harley Street doctor, regarding William's inability to father a child." Grange raised both hands. "Do not ask me for inappropriate details. It was dated just under a year before Alfred was born. Silas was born a few weeks later, and it was William that brought the doctor. I can only surmise that some arrangement was made. It never crossed my mind to reveal what had happened."

Col Grange was disregarding etiquette and puffing on his long-stemmed pipe even though ladies were present. Both his daughters had agreed that the circumstances allowed it.

"I didn't need my brother's properties, and I had no interest in his title. There wasn't any money worth speaking of. I hope neither of you feel I should have acted otherwise." He furrowed his brow, looking at Anne and Lydia in turn.

Anne privately thought that seeing Alfred disinherited would have been quite acceptable, and that the town house in Bristol would have been a rather jolly place to live, sans her aunt, but on reflection, her father had clearly done the only thing possible to save not only the Grange family but Silas and his mother from a terrible scandal. And she rather liked Frances, who had insisted that Burnton Cary must be sold.

"We'll say no more about it. It isn't a fit subject for young ladies to speak of."

"It's a little late for that, Father," said Lydia. "We do need to clear one thing up, at least."

"I don't know if she killed Samuel, if that's what you're driving at."

"Why would she?"

The colonel sighed and pulled at his pipe. "William having died intestate, all routine payments from his accounts were stopped by the bank. Lettie had a very small allowance. She could not have afforded to keep the payments up, and nor could she have known that I would take them over, as I wasn't supposed to know anything about it.

It was only after Samuel ran away that I made the decision to pay the stipend to Maud myself - the poor woman had enough troubles. I might have told Lettie, eventually, but I didn't wish to cause her the embarrassment of discovering that I knew what she'd done, or to have her worry that I might dispute Alfred's inheriting William's estate."

"So Samuel confronted Aunt Lettie and she *killed* him?"

"He might have confronted her," said Anne. "I don't know. She said, when she was raving, 'I meant to. I just wasn't certain that I had.' I suppose we'll never know."

"In any case," the colonel said, extinguishing his pipe and reaching for his hat. "As I said, we'll say no more about it. Alfred and Frances will have finished with the vicar, and the cortège is waiting."

Anne paused in front of the hall mirror and adjusted her hat. She didn't know what had stopped her from saving Lettie. Perhaps a sense of justice; let the guilty fall. Perhaps only the fact that she had never loved Lettie, who had made such a very bad job of replacing her mother. Perhaps, she thought wryly, she'd been too shy. Too *mousy*. She smiled to herself. She was one of life's observers, always had been. She stepped over the worn threshold of the old house, with its peeling paint, and was glad to feel the door slamming shut behind her.

As the carriage passed the garden wall, she could see Silas, tipping a barrow load of leaves onto the fire that burned in the same spot it had when Lettie died. Atop the fire was the Guy she and Frances had made. The thing had sat in the scullery since Guy Fawkes night. Frances had thrust it at Silas earlier, and instructed him to burn it. Why she cared, Anne had no idea, but it had apparently mattered enough to bring tears to her eyes as she'd held it out. Somehow the effigy had regained its hat.

Silas, she supposed, should really have been with them. It was a family-only funeral, but Silas was her half-cousin, Alfred's half-brother. He was one of them, for better or ill. But then again, he was nothing to Lettie. He was better off where he was, she decided, and made certain not to think about whether the family owed him, or his mother, anything more.

The fire, doused with the lamp oil no doubt, ran quickly up the sides of the Guy and fizzed joyfully as it ate its way through the old feathers of Aunt Lettie's precious bird hat. The birds shook and trembled on their wires, a nest of flames surrounding them. *Like phoenixes* thought Anne, but they were just dead yellow songbirds, with their stuffing full of dust. Let them go. Let it all go.

She pressed her hands together in a prayerful position, feeling the pressure of fingertip to fingertip. The house passed from view, and they went to lay Aunt Lettie in the dank, seeping ground.

January 5th

Twelfth Night

Peter Sutton

The ghost flees across Kochlias and I follow. The city's stygian and labyrinthine streets abetting its escape. All ghosts flee; I wonder where to? If I could collect this one, maybe, maybe I would be ready for Twelfth Night. There is a clatter ahead and, as I careen around the corner, a fathomless cloud of brick dust obscures my view. The ghost's light is lost within the ashen miasma. I yank my scarf, the same colour as the dust, the same colour as my clothes, over my mouth, squint through my eyelashes and slow, to penetrate the gloom of the alleyway.

There is another clangour and my feet are drawn towards the pandemonium. I step out into a main thoroughfare, the mouth of the alley blowing particulates into an already gathered crowd of the Tenebrous.

I have lost the ghost, but the crowd waits expectantly. Here and there amongst the black figures is one in grey, another of the Crepuscular, my own kind. The wide road curves out of sight to both the left and the right but, where the alley has disgorged me, there is a small square. A lone yew tree stands central. Its branches reach to a balcony, upon which profligate light spills.

Fingers of shadow entwine upon the cobbles and the noise of the crowd peaks and is replaced with a hush. There is a flash as a door opens; one of the Illuminated is going to address the crowd.

The white-clad figure, extravagantly lit, contemptuous of the resentment running through the crowd like a contagion, raises its arms and throws back its hood. The blond head revealed, the alabaster face imperious.

"People of Kochlias. Third night is upon us. Who amongst you has the requisite amount of Obol to enter the Lottery?" Hands like marble grip the balcony and the avaricious hawk-like expression sweeps the crowd. None volunteer. None have the Obol yet. It is too early.

The murmuring starts, impossible to pinpoint where in the crowd. Eventually, as it has the other times I have witnessed the Illuminated address the populace, there are cries of "Beneficence, Beneficence!" But the Illuminated guard their light jealously. The door opens and closes, the square returns to darkness. The crowd, no longer bound with common purpose, breaks into clots and the Tenebrous scurry to regain their lairs before the Corone enforce curfew.

I share a glance with my fellow grey-clad Crepuscular cousins before we too scamper off to our roosts, a step above the Tenebrous, but way below the Illuminated. I turn to where the alleyway was, but it has closed over, the reconfiguration of Kochlias's ways a constant refinement.

I make my way home, but first I must visit the wife and children; a trip to the Tenebrous ghetto.

When the cobbles turn to hard-packed dirt and the slate walls turn to raven-black pumice - there is the home of my wife. I do not knock.

"Husband! Have you Bronze for us?" she greets me, as though I was expected. One of the children has espied my approach no doubt.

"Hello, my wife. There is no Bronze to spare in this, the Twelfth month." I unwind my scarf and clap dust from my ragged cloak.

"Yet you have enough to purchase Crepuscular robes?" she demands.

"We discussed this. Remember?"

She shakes her head. It is hard for the Tenebrous; it was not such a long time ago that I was such. The gleam of words, subordinate to what I may command now I have access to some light.

"I am to go first. Only the Crepuscular can enter the Lottery," I state. She nods, in agreement, or submission, it matters not. Soon, one more ghost, maybe two, soon, I may have enough Obol to enter the Lottery.

I share the scraps I can spare, then take my leave whilst they eat, whilst they are distracted, before their pitifulness can stop me, make me spend the Obol on them. Their forgetfulness, when I am out of sight, my only consolation. Their base state disgusts me, disturbs me; I still pity them yet, but less each time I visit. They could help themselves, I sometimes feel.

I return home. The streets of Kochlias are in a playful mood. It must be the excitement of the Twelfth month. It takes me longer to traverse the ways than usual and I stop at the bridge for long moments, hoping to catch sight of the Illuminated maiden once more upon her marble balcony. High above the streets in the airy heights she wanders. I watch and wait, but there is no sight of her. The Illuminated close their shutters and their imprecation of darkness sweeps across Kochlias. I have almost left it too late – I hurry home whilst the Corone are loosed. I make it back just before curfew.

***

The ghost has nowhere to go. My trap arcs through the air and lands at its base. Its light is snatched out of the air. The gunmetal body of the trap steams gently as I extract the Obol. I am lucky. It is sixth day. The meagre availability of ghosts, hunted to scarcity, means the only way to get the requisite Obols is to take them from another hunter. I watch for other Crepuscular with trepidation now. The few Tenebrous that attempt to get enough Obol to join the ranks of the Crepuscular thin the ghosts even more.

I count the Obol sewn into my robes, one each end of the scarf, one at the end of the hood, two in the hem, one in the armpit, three in my belt. I contemplate spending one on a weapon, but dismiss the idea. Speed and cunning are my weapons, and my shield. My musings end as I secure the trap back onto my belt. I scan the alleyway in which I have wound up: a part of Kochlias I don't recognise, the sere walls sloping down, the cobble obscured with filth. I take the path downwards until it winds and limps to the city wall.

I place my hand upon the wall, then rest my head against it and close my eyes. The susurrus beyond scrapes across my listening mind. I grind my teeth and shake my head. Enough! First the Lottery and if, only if, I then am elevated to Illuminated, I can drag the wife and children with me. Before I may even think of the Ferryman.

***

The fact there are two of them throws me. Two Crepuscular working together, one chasing me into the arms of the second. I stumble to a halt and spin to meet the first, the chaser. The other leaps forward and grapples me, but, as I surmised, has no weapon. The first is more dangerous, armed with a sickle blade.

As he approaches, I go limp, making the one holding me take all my weight. As he adjusts, I spring up and back and arch my head, so the crunch of his nose is gristly music in my ears.

My head rings but he has let go enough for me to spin him into the path of the blade. The shink, as it scrapes a rib, sets my teeth on edge. I pull the trap, its dull grey body a shadow in the alleyway, and spin it overhead. The stabbed man slides to the ground. The trap whistles through the air and connects, with a crack. The head of the man with the blade blooms a halo of blood. He drops, a puppet with cut strings.

There is a whispering and the ghost that leaps forth from the first body shines brightly, far more brightly than the ghosts I have been hunting. I deploy the trap and the ghost is sucked, screaming silently, within. I crouch over the other, who breathes shallowly. I take his blade.

I extract the Obol, three whole coins, more, much more than the ghosts of the Tenebrous. A slick of blood gathers at the tip of the blade and a drop falls to the cobbles. Him or me, I mutter. I think this night's work has brought me enough Obol to enter the Lottery. I even have enough to exchange one for Bronze, to share with my wife. Enough to tide her over until I can collect the family to me? I tell myself it is.. I resent having to pay them now, though. She could help herself.

***

An expectant hush falls upon the crowd. I grip the handle of the sickle until the grain is imprinted upon my palm. It is the same Illuminated that addresses the crowd, or one so alike it makes no difference.

"People of Kochlias. Eighth night is upon us. Who amongst you has the requisite amount of Obol to enter the Lottery?"

I raise my hand, one fatly gleaming Obol within it, there is shuffling all around me. I pull out the sickle and sweep the crowd with a stare, teeth bared. I turn in a complete circle. They mutter, the Tenebrous; the few Crepuscular move towards me.

There is another Obol held aloft deep in the crowd. The murmuration shifting, roiling. The Corone muscle their way through, dressed in their feathered cloaks; knobbed staves prod and poke the crowd out of the way. I endure the avaricious stink of the crowd, as a way is opened up for me to the yew tree.

The other Crepuscular with enough Obol is a woman. As she leaves the edge of the crowd, the Corone open a circle keeping the crowd at bay with wood; she is spat upon by one of the Tenebrous. The man, or woman, who spat is clubbed to the ground, the grunts of the Corone administering the punishment loud in the sudden hush.

The ghost that springs up is dim, but worth a fraction of an Obol. It spins for a brief second, casting ruby, then emerald light upon the front rank of the crowd, but none have a trap. I finger mine but am unsure of the protocol. It leaps away and, from the crowd, two Crepuscular give chase.

We are led up steps carved into the tree, along the wide branch, and onto the balcony. Set against the wall is a model of Kochlias. I glance at its round, labyrinthine shape, the steady pulse of changing streets somehow, marvellously, tracked within. I determine to study it later and concentrate on our host.

The illuminated is androgynous, beautiful, icy, imperious. It raises its chin and the Corone that stands near grunts, "Obol."

I spend a minute gathering them into one pile; the female Crepuscular withdraws a bag from between her breasts. We hand them over; their light, bright in the shadows below, barely add to the extravagance displayed here on the balcony.

The Illuminated takes one from each pile and then adds the rest to a cloth bag hanging from its hip, tied with golden ribbon. It nods to the Corone, who bows. Unsure of the etiquette still, I also bow. The female stands contemptuous of any ceremony.

The Illuminated withdraws through the door. I take a step forward and a hand, much larger than my own, clamps upon my shoulder. I turn to look up into the Corone's face. His bushy beard is split in a white grin. He shakes his head. I glance at the female. She is watching with interest.

If there is some signal I do not catch it, but the Corone lets me go, my shoulder burning from his grip. He grunts again, I do not catch what he says but it is obvious he wants us to follow him.

Inside the marbled residence are many lamps. We shade our eyes; how many Obol does it take to provide so much light? I wonder if I should have tried for one more Obol; I push thoughts of my wife and children from my mind.

We follow the silent Corone, and I marvel at his soundless grace - so large a man, so economical in movement, a dangerous opponent without any doubt. He leads us down corridors, down steps, along more corridors and, eventually, out into a circular room open to the sky. We have walked far, never once having to resort to the streets; the Illuminated have their own ways.

Effulgent torches shine upon something I have never beheld before: a collection of flora, deliberately planted; a profusion of greens, and browns, and reds, and yellows. Nestled within is a contraption that spurts water and the space is full of its tinkling sound.

My eyes, used to the shadows and gloom of the streets are aching, my cheeks wet from a cascade of tears. The other Crepuscular equally affected. The Corone not.

"Rest," his gruff voice commands. "Wait."

He turns on his heel and glides from the courtyard. I turn to the female but she has already scurried off and taken position on a bench. I follow. She watches me through narrowed eyes.

"What do you think will happen now?" I ask

She shrugs.

"Do you think there'll be more Crepuscular coming?"

She watches me, impassive.

"Here, I mean. More entrants to the Lottery?"

Her expression doesn't change. She hugs herself, the hostility of her gaze makes me smile sadly and shuffle over to a different bench. I finger the sickle inside my sleeve.

There is a sudden burst of piping notes and a bird, small as a starling, drab in colour, hops about and lands in the water. Fascinated, I watch it clean itself. It is so seldom that anything with animation is seen upon the streets. The Tenebrous consume anything that dares.

"Little scamp." The melodious voice shocks me to my feet. I whirl, blade half-pulled. The Illuminated stands an arm's-length from me. I hadn't heard any approach.

"I beg your pardon?" I ask. Aware that the female has crept closer, putting me between her and the Illuminated.

"The bird. He is a playful one."

I don't know what to say, so remain silent, as does the female.

"You must be weary. You are ahead of most of the competition, so have a chance to rest before the Lottery on Twelfth Night. Your entry is assured." The Illuminated claps twice and two women, dressed unlike any I have seen - in short olive tunics and beige leggings - hurry into the courtyard. One takes my hand, the other the female's.

"These servants will take you to a chamber where you may rest, be washed and made ready." The Illuminated makes small flicking motions with both hands and we are led away separately.

***

It is Twelfth Night. I am dressed in loincloth, armed with sword and buckler and brimming with anticipation.

The apartment has a massive bed, a couch, a sunken bath, filled with hot water whenever I want it, and torches, lamps and lanterns. It has learning for the taking. It has no windows and but one door. Which has remained closed.

I have been washed, my robes removed, my sickle taken away, I have slept, and eaten and paced, confined to an opulent prison until now. The servants are solicitous, but uncommunicative. Unable to go forth, or find out more, I have stewed. There are only so many baths you can take. I am mad with silence and inactivity.

Outside, the once silent corridors now bustle. I have previously only heard sweet singing down them, and nothing more. There is now a great activity.

Upon waking, I immediately spotted the sword and buckler. I am now armed. I sit and watch the door.

There is a clunk, a ratcheting sound behind me and I turn to see the wall retreating. I stand and face it. Beyond is a large space, dusty ground. No, not dust, something coarser. Sand? I creep to the edge and look out.

In the great round space more rooms are opening, like mine. Above is a great glinting expanse of glass. Behind it, light, the Illuminated.

Lottery.

I tense and relax muscles and stretch so that my back pops and cracks. I stalk into the arena, noting eleven others also making their entrances. Only one will walk out of here; to join the Illuminated.

A bear of a man roars and charges his nearest neighbour. I hear the clash of steel upon steel from another quarter and slowly circle, trying to keep my neighbours in sight.

The nearest, a youngster, first fuzz on his face, stalks closer then takes up a fighting pose, and hop-steps nearer. I am ready. The clash of his sword upon my buckler drowns out the sounds of fighting from further away. I try to look in many directions at once. We exchange a couple of blows. He favours the right. After one such exchange, my sword clattering harmlessly from the boss of his shield; I take a chance and slam the edge of my buckler into his face.

He isn't ready for such a tactic. It scores a deep gash and his head whips to the side, crunching bone loud, spray of blood upon the sand. My following blade takes him high in the chest. He stiffens and drops. I finish him off with a stab to the throat.

A wall rumbles closed. His ghost is child-like and flashes briefly before winking out. This whole area is a ghost-trap, I realise.

I scan the battleground. Near me are two women, seemingly evenly matched. I stride towards them, trying to come up from their side. I guess they'll both spot me.

The first, her grey hair loose, sweat-slicked so that she must wipe it from her eyes, crab-walks away. The other, slimmer, taller, tries to match her, they both try to put the other between them and me.

I reach the first, the slimmer one, and she cannot fight us both off. She tries to skip backwards and catches my blade on her buckler, but the other nips forward and her sword takes the slim woman in the leg.

I feint and the slim woman goes to block, but my blade, that I fake toward her, goes sideways and pierces her opponent's 's throat. She topples to the ground. I jump back to avoid the other woman's blade. The ghost distracts neither of us for long. The blood coursing down her leg and soaking into the sand gives me an advantage that I fully exploit.

She manages to graze me, a stinging slash on one cheek that bleeds freely, before I finish her with a stab through the stomach and another through the heart. Her ghost is brief in its radiance.

I am blowing at this point, and hope that I have a little time to catch my breath. There is no other sound of fighting. I have been vaguely aware of other flashes, other walls rumbling closed. I gaze around the arena. The female from

Eighth day and the bear of a man stand in the distance. He has made short work of four opponents and the woman has accounted for two more; with the three I have killed that leaves just us.

The woman looks from me, to the larger man, shrugs and makes her way to him; he is slightly closer. I stalk towards them both.

He is massive, muscular, well-fed; may have been a Crepuscular for a long time? He moves with practised grace and I narrow my eyes; it is familiar. Shorn of the ceremonial mask, the leather and the feather cloak, he is nevertheless the Corone. The Illuminated have stacked the competition!

The woman dances away from a charge and I see her glance wildly to me. She's spotted it too. With no word exchanged, we work in concert. The Corone senses the change, and backs slowly away, his sword atop his buckler, defensive.

I go right, she goes left. I kick the sand towards him, a fake-out. He is not drawn in by it. She drops her sword. What is she doing? He spots it, of course, and moves towards her, I take a few steps, within range of his sword. Still moving towards the woman, he swipes me. I easily block.

He is a few steps away from her, and half-concentrating on me. The buckler she throws slams into his skull with a clang. It is all the opening I need and hop towards him. Some instinct sees my thrust thwarted. Instead of taking him in the heart, he manages to deflect it enough that it takes him in the arm. A second blade slices, and he somehow manages to block hers too. Yet his sword clatters from his grasp.

As I pull back, readying another blow, he launches an unexpected punch. A massive fist like a boulder catches me and I feel a rib, possibly two, pop. His buckler deflects my blow, but hers takes him through the eye. He topples, like some hewn tree, and her sword is wrenched from her hand. His ghost is like a starling's wing, vast and multifaceted. It sweeps across the arena, before it too winks out. I take a breath filled with broken glass and a short step sees my blade slice through the woman's stomach.

She falls. I limp over and raise my sword. I grimace.

"Please..." she says.

I freeze.

"My daughter," she coughs. "Please save my daughter."

A dying wish? I curse it but know I will comply.

I kneel and she whispers instructions. I have no need to finish her off; her blood takes the shapes of wings beneath her dying body. When she has gone, and her ghost spirals and flits away, I stand; my broken ribs, like betrayer's daggers, stab me.

I am ready.

White rose petals shower down. Their cloying aroma sickens me. They turn pink where they touch the blood upon the sand. I drop my sword, fumble the buckler from my arm and trudge back to my luxurious cage.

***

Servants wash me, bind my wounds and then leave me. I fall asleep whilst I wait.

I awake to light, the same androgynous Illuminated sits eating fruit at my table when I get up.

"Welcome to the One Hundred," s/he says.

"I won?" I wondered.

"Do you not remember? Twelfth Night is over. The One Hundred are complete again. Kochlias is back to normal." His/her long slim fingers play over the surface of the ruby-gold apple. S/he takes a delicate bite. "Do you want to see your demesne?" s/he says.

I nod.

S/he stands and bids me follow. We take a long walk through the Illuminated's ways. I am still in loincloth only. We meet no-one.

"Why is it so empty?" I ask.

S/he arches a perfectly-shaped golden eyebrow. "Why? Because we wish it to be so."

"But all this space," I say.

S/he stops, looks around at the corridors stretching into the distance, the massive, empty room we are passing, a multitude of doors standing open upon it.

"What space?" S/he asks, then carries on. I follow.

The rooms the Illuminated takes me to are as large as the great square with the yew tree. Seven servants, grey haired, kneel and bow, heads to the floor.

"Why are they kneeling?" I ask.

"You may rise," the Illuminated says.

The servants rise and splinter, moving off in several directions. Two come back immediately and drape me in Illuminated's robes. I finger the soft and silken white material.

"Thank you," I murmur. The servants share a startled look and the Illuminated arches an eyebrow. I curse myself for forgetting my new station.

The woman from the arena was dead, her dying wish binding. My servants seem old; I could clearly use a new one.

"Come," s/he says and leads me to the floor-to-ceiling window which s/he pushes open so that we may walk out upon the balcony.

I look down and see the bridge, where I have spent so long looking up to this very window. Across it, and along the streets, Tenebrous scurry.

"It was her?"

"Who? Oh this demesne? Yes, it was a woman who owned it previously. Before she accumulated enough wealth to pay the Ferryman. To start her new life."

I nod. It is my plan too, has been ever since I discovered the tales.

"I have obligations," I say.

"Obligations?"

"My family. The daughter of another."

The illuminated purses its lips and looks a question.

"I need them brought here," I say and turn to look out across Kochlias, to the slums shrouded in constant shadow, filthy with smoke.

"It will cost you," the Illuminated says.

I contemplate the drop below me. I gaze across the city, I notice how clean it is here, how light.

"Of course it will."

I wonder if it is worth it. The wife has enough to live on for some time; I was generous with my last act of charity. Perhaps, with the largess of my demesne, I could still be generous. Pass her word that she now needed to help herself. Put the children to work. My chance of a new life, gathering a Ferryman's fare, that's what's important now. "How much does this demesne make?" I ask.

The Illuminated shrugs.

"What happens now?"

The Illuminated laughs, a high cascading, musical sound. "Now you learn to live." S/he gently turns me away from the sights and smells of Kochlias. "Welcome to the ranks of the Illuminated," s/he says.

December 23rd

Tom Bawcock's Eve

Chrissey Harrison

As aich we'd clunk, E's health we drunk, in bumpers bremmen high,
And when up caame Tom Bawcock's name, We'd prais'd 'un to the sky

Though most of the village sang along, the deep tones of the male voice choir resonated above the general chorus; deep, rich and full of genuine pride and joy. Marie could barely understand the words of the song, but she'd worked out that the same verse, repeated over and over, told the story of the Cornish village of Mousehole's ancestral hero. The air, dense with drizzle, refracted the light from the Christmas decorations into misty halos, on this night before Christmas Eve.

The heart of the celebration wound its way through the cobbled streets. Marie hovered on the fringe, trying to keep out of the way. She'd barely lived in the village a week and felt as though she were intruding on this special moment. Like it should be private. She wasn't the only outsider and, technically, she was far less 'outside' than the tourists taking blurry snaps of the village's unique Christmas lights. But, maybe that was it, she felt like a fraud, her grey woollen coat a disguise to blend in with the locals. Maybe she'd feel less like an imposter in a neon cagoule.

She could have stayed home, of course, but she was intrigued by this strange custom. Everyone she'd met in the village had been keen to share the tale of Tom Bawcock, the brave fisherman who, four hundred years ago, saved the village from starvation by sailing out in a dreadful storm to catch fish.

Along the road, bobbing paper lanterns approached and the villagers closed ranks to watch the procession. The choir launched into another round with rosy-cheeked gusto.

Merry place you may believe, Tiz Mouzel 'pon Tom Bawcock's eve
To be there then who wouldn't wesh, to sup o' sibm soorts o' fish
When morgy brath had cleared the path, Comed lances for a fry
And then us had a bit o' scad an' Starry-gazie pie

Marie looked for a way through to the pub, The Ship Inn. She was thirsty and the rain was damp and uncomfortable. Plus, she'd been told on several occasions that she had to try the Stargazy pie —whatever that was– that they'd be serving at the pub. It was a big part of the celebration and she harboured the secret hope that partaking might baptise her into true villager-hood. But, she didn't want to be rude by pushing through, so she settled for watching the procession.

"Oh, aren't they cute," an old lady beside her said. "That's my granddaughter over there."

Marie peered at the group of children bearing the paper lanterns. Again, not wanting to be rude she politely asked, "which one?"

"On the right, there, with the fishes."

The little girl in question held a paper construction of stacked fish, seven of them, glowing with fairy lights inside.

"Do I know you, my dear?" the old lady asked.

An embarrassed heat flushed her cheeks. "Oh, probably not. I'm staying in the cottage on Peony street."

"Oh, you're the young lady related to Mrs Batton what passed away, God rest her. What a pleasure. Welcome to Mouzel!" The woman offered Marie a hug, which she accepted stiffly, worried something in her posture would offend.

"I do hope you'll be poppin' round our coffee morning." She paused to wave at her grand-daughter. Marie waved too, to join in.

"Coffee morning?"

"On the Saturday after Christmas, at the village hall. Come have a natter and a cuppa tea, give us a chance to welcome you to the village proper."

"Oh, well, maybe."

The lady's granddaughter came running over, her fish lantern swishing about and catching more than a few surprised elbows.

"Did you see, Nanny?"

Marie took the opportunity to slip away, afraid that if she stuck around she'd have to answer more questions and people would start to see her for what she was; some townie playing house in the country. It had been frightening enough, moving all this way, leaving everything she'd known for over a decade, but she figured a tiny village like this would be a good place to get lost. When she'd arrived, she found herself the primary topic of gossip; it turned out it was impossible to be invisible in a place so small.

The singers came to the end of another round of the *Ballad of Tom Bawcock* and there was a pause, which Marie experienced as an awkward silence. As she stood there, the feeling that people were staring, whispering, crept over her like a slimy itch and she had an intense urge to be alone.

She escaped through fleeting gaps in the crowd, down towards the wall that looked out over the harbour. A glowing sea monster undulated in jerky steps. Each section of its sinuous body lit up in turn to make it look as if it were swimming though the water. The Mousehole Christmas lights were wonderfully creative. She watched the bobbing sea monster with her eyes slightly unfocused, letting it become a blur.

The creature of light wriggled away through the water and Marie blinked. A prickle of adrenalin. She looked around to see if anyone else had seen it, but there was no-one else there. When she looked back the sea monster was still there, blinking lights giving the illusion of motion and nothing more. It must have been a ripple on the surface.

A hand reached in front of her and set down a paper bowl with a plastic fork jutting up from the middle. Fish-scented steam wafted up and Marie inhaled deeply. She glanced sideways.

"A bit o' Stargazy pie for yer," said the stranger beside her.

She looked back down at the bowl of fish and pastry. There were lumps of potato and onion in there, and a thick, creamy sauce. It smelled delicious and set her mouth watering.

"Thank you."

"Yer welcome." The man folded his arms on the wall and stared out across the harbour. The light sparkled off drops of moisture caught in his grey and grizzled beard. He wore a heavy coat over the top of a thick woollen shirt and braces, and a traditional cap.

Not sure what else to say, Marie took a small bite of pie and savoured the taste. "It's good."

"They's fresh caught local pilchards," he said, by way of an explanation, in his broad Cornish accent.

The first mouthful had set her stomach rumbling. She hadn't realised how hungry she was. She loaded another forkful and blew on it to cool it down.

Maybe because he didn't say anything, just stood there quietly looking out to sea, Marie felt unaccountably comfortable in the stranger's presence. Whatever thoughts were going on behind those crow-footed eyes, they were bigger than her and her problems. Her concerns about what people thought of her suddenly seemed insignificant.

"Why do they call it Stargazy pie?" she asked.

"Cos the fishes be lookin' up at the stars. They puts the heads and tails through the crust you see."

"Oh." She poked around in her dish for a head but thankfully didn't find one. Or a tail for that matter.

"You must be new to these parts."

"Yes." That awkward sense of being an impostor resurfaced along with an uncomfortable warmth in her gut.

"Ain't nought wrong with that. Even ol' Tom were a newcomer once."

"Sorry?"

"Ol' Tom Bawcock, what they be singing the song of," he gestured with a nod back towards the villagers clustering around the pub.

She turned to face him while she ate the pie. "How could you know that? The story I heard made it sound like he'd always lived here."

"Well, Tom were a travelling man in his youth. Took a wife here he did, and settled down, and that was how he came to be a man o' Mouzel."

"I hadn't heard that part. You must know the story better than anyone."

"That I do." He fell silent for a moment, eyes drifting away to another time and place. A place of sorrow, perhaps. Marie searched for another subject. Something about this man fascinated her. She could see in that weathered face a richness of experience, and felt enriched herself just for being near it.

"Are you a fisherman?"

"All my life," he said, wistfully. "'Tis the only life."

"I've never been fishing," Marie confessed. It seemed everyone in Mousehole fished, or lived with someone who did. That was part of why she felt so out of place here. It was a way of life totally alien to her. "I've never even been in a boat before."

The stranger turned to her with a look of incredulity on his face. "Never been in a boat!"

Marie shook her head as she polished off the last of her pie.

"Well, mayhap we can fix that, at least."

"Sorry?"

He pushed off from the wall and held out a gnarled and calloused hand. "Would the lovely lady join me for a tour of the bay?"

Marie opened her mouth to turn him down, but something stopped her. Maybe she should go with him. Before she could speak she found herself taking his hand. His palm was warm and rough.

"If yer to live in Mouzel you'd ought least to see it once the way Ol' Tom did, all them years ago. From the sea."

She followed him down the steps towards the boats moored in the sheltered harbour. He escorted her to a small, weathered fishing boat, with a red painted hull and a white cabin near the stern. She stepped over the gap between the pontoon and the boat, clinging tightly to the stranger's arm with one hand and gripping the metal rail with the other. She could see the black water lapping at the planks, like it anticipated her falling.

Once she was across, he followed, hopping nimbly for a man of his years. He released a few ropes while Marie tried to keep out of the way. Then he disappeared into the tiny cabin and started up a throaty engine. Water chugged at the rear of the boat and they began to turn slowly away from the pontoon until they faced the narrow gap in the harbour wall. The 'mousehole' the village was named for. The boat picked up speed and Marie crouched down. The edge of the boat was too low, barely up to her knees, and she felt sure she'd pitch over the side if she wasn't careful. She inched her way towards the prow, with one hand on the rail, while the glowing Christmas lights of the harbour slipped past.

The lights danced on the water, creating luminous fish which seemed to dart beneath the surface. Just a trick of the light, but they seemed to move so fluidly that Marie reached out to touch them and they scattered away from her hand, darting away, down into the depths. Marie snatched her hand back, but, when she looked again, the reflections simply rippled on the surface.

Soon they were passing through the harbour wall. Beyond, the sea stretched out, inky-black and eternal. Where the choppy water of the bay met the millpond stillness of the harbour the boat quivered and jumped. But, once they were beyond the gap the vessel rode over the waves smoothly, slicing through the small wavelets and gliding out into the darkness. Even the chug of the engine seemed to fade away.

The air out here was clean and fresh, heavy with the salt richness of the sea. As the harbour wall and the merry lights of Mousehole retreated behind them. Marie wondered if she should be afraid to let this stranger take her off into the night, but she wasn't. She felt only a profound sense of peace and wonder at the vastness of the sea.

She loosened her nervous grip on the rail and ran her hand along it, but snatched it back when something pinched. She checked her palm and tugged out a splinter. She could have sworn the rail was metal, painted red like the hull, but now she felt rough, weathered wood. She blinked and looked again, it *was* smooth red paint, cool metal, but a moment ago...

The bow of the small boat speared through a wave and threw a handful of spray into Marie's face. She leaned back from the edge and wiped her face with her sleeve. Her stomach lurched as the boat dipped into a trough between waves. A stiff breeze had sprung up and stirred the light drizzle into a haze.

A spot of water hit her forehead. Was it starting to rain in earnest, or was that just more spray? She looked up to where the sky now roiled with angry black clouds, darkening by the second. They were sailing straight out into a storm.

"Hey?" she called. "Is this safe?"

A flash of lightning lanced the sky, followed almost immediately by a crack of thunder that resonated through her chest like a physical blow. Marie curled into a ball in the bow and held on as the boat pitched and rolled through the growing swell.

"Shouldn't we go back?"

The light from the cabin went out, plunging Marie into a disorienting, absolute darkness. All she could feel was the wood of the boat below her which moved so much now it was of little comfort. While she lay there, hoping her eyes would adjust, another flash of lightning lit up the sky. It left a ghostly after image in her eyes. The sky growled with another rumble of thunder and the heavens opened. Rain fell in sheets, pelting the surface of the water so hard it raised a deafening roar. A stab of fear gripped Marie.

She needed to get to the cabin. Releasing her death grip, she put her hand out to feel her way along the deck but came down instead on a nest of tangled rope. Had that been there before? Was she still in the bow or had she moved somehow? It was so hard to keep her bearings when she could hardly see. She got her feet under her and cautiously stood, but kept her hands on the splintered timber of the boat and started to inch her way along.

With the next flash of lightning she saw the man standing in the middle of the vessel, his face shadowed by the wide hood of an oilskin cloak. Startled, Marie stepped backwards and the back of her leg collided with a bench that spanned the width of the boat. She lost her balance and sat down heavily. The silhouette of the man lingered in her vision for a moment. Where was the cabin, the metal railing around the stern, the radio mast? She held her breath, waiting for her eyes to pick up on some hint of light.

Then a warm glow pushed the darkness back. She saw the man now crouched over a small lantern. He lowered the glass cover and the flame grew a little brighter. In the soft light Marie could see the end of an oar stuck up at the side of the boat and the rain pooling in the bottom of the rounded hull. What was going on? How could this be a different boat? But it was clearly smaller and wooden and crammed full of nets and baskets.

"How is this possible?" she asked under her breath, not really expecting an answer. Everything, including the man in front of her suddenly felt so unreal. She looked down at her hands and clothes. Her jeans and wool coat were gone. Instead she found a rough wool dress and the heavy weight of a cloak draped around her shoulders. Her nails felt chipped, her skin chapped.

The man suddenly lunged towards her and she flinched. But he only reached past her to grab the rope net she'd touched before and began to lay it out along the boat.

"Who are you? What is this?"

Suddenly he looked at her and she jumped. Everything had seemed so strange she'd begun to wonder if it was a dream and she half expected that he couldn't hear her.

"Come on, Aggie. Quicker we land a catch, quicker we can be home and dryin' out." He pointed to the end of net near her feet.

In something of a daze, Marie crouched and took hold of the rope. It felt scratchy and real against her palms. It had to be a hallucination. There'd been drugs in that fish pie he'd given her and now she was seeing things, that was it! But, everything felt so real. The rain seeping in through the wool of the dress certainly felt real, as did the wind and rain biting at her cheeks.

"On three." The man said. "One, two..."

Marie's attention snapped back to the net in her hand. Maybe, if she played out this strange fantasy, things would go back to normal.

"Three." Between them they cast the net over the side, but Marie's end twisted and didn't open up over the water.

"What were that?" The man said with a sigh. "Good thing there ain't no other souls crazy as us out here as could see that, else they'd all be talking about how Ol' Tom's daughter can't even throw a net. I'd ne'er live it down." He chuckled; a strangely warm sound in the cold, stormy night.

He hauled the net back in and spread it out ready once more. It was heavier now that the fibres were clogged with seawater. This time, when they threw the net it opened out into a wide circle. The boat dipped on the one side and Marie's stomach lurched with it. She crouched and gripped tight to the gunwale of the vessel. But, even with the rolling waves, the little boat righted itself easily and bobbed along, quite stable. The weighted edges of the net sank and Tom gestured to the trailing ropes. Marie released her grip on the boat to take hold.

They hauled in the net, filled with wriggling fish, and dumped it into the bottom of the boat. Marie felt the writhing mass around her ankles. There were so many! So many for one small net, and all different types too. Maybe that was why they were fishing in this terrible storm instead of heading for the safety of the harbour.

Marie suddenly realised what she was seeing. This was the story she'd heard all day! The story the celebrations in Mousehole were all about; brave Tom Bawcock, the fisherman who'd gone out to sea in a dangerous storm to find food for his starving village. But, the story had been very clear that Old Tom Bawcock had gone alone. There was no mention of a daughter. Was this some bizarre, alternate reality she was playing out?

She realised Tom was busy untangling fish from the net and making it ready to throw again. She ran her hands over the rough fibres until she encountered a slick, squirming body. It was hard to see in the low light, with the rain dripping off the cowl of her hood but, mainly by feel, she managed to free the fish. She held it briefly before it squirmed free and landed in the bottom of the hull with the rest of the catch. Once they'd cleared the net they tossed it into the water again to draw in another batch.

Marie found herself absorbed in the experience, fascinated. For a time the dreadful weather became no more than a dramatic backdrop to this scene she was playing out, and she could imagine she really was Tom's daughter. Who was this girl? Marie imagined her as courageous and determined, sure-footed and strong. She felt the idea of her, inside. There was even laughter to be had amid the squall, when a small fish shot from her hands and flipped its tail in her face. For just a while, in this most alien of situations, this surreal hallucination, she felt right. Accepted.

"One more," Tom announced, as they readied the net a final time. While they were waiting for the weights to sink, the boat suddenly spun sideways, hit by a freak wave, and sent both of them stumbling. Tom staggered backwards and stepped on a sliding fish. His foot shot out from under him, and he collapsed backwards into the mass of nets and baskets in the stern. His end of the rope pulled from his hand and slithered over the side. The net began to drift away on the swell.

Marie kept hold of her end as the waves tried to tear it from her grasp. It dragged her towards the edge of the boat. The coarse rope pulled through her hands, burning her palms.

"Let it go!" Tom yelled as he struggled to untangle himself.

"I've got it," her knees hit the gunwale and she tried to brace herself there. Right now she was Tom's daughter, and she didn't think Tom's daughter would have been the type to let go. A moment later, when the boat lurched over a large wave and rocked to one side she pitched forward. Her heart stopped for a moment. The water seemed to rise up to meet her in slow motion. She tried to twist around as she fell and saw Tom reaching for her. She thrust out her hand towards him but her hand passed through his as if it wasn't even there.

When the shock of hitting the icy water cleared, Marie struggled back to the surface and gasped down salty air.

"Agatha!" She could hear Tom calling, his voice filled with terror and pain.

"Here!" Marie tried to call back, but a wave slapped into her face and she ended up coughing and spitting instead. She caught a glimpse of Tom holding the lantern high, scanning the water, his face pale and wide eyed, before a tall wave lifted her up and bore her away from him. The swell twisted her round and in the distance she saw torches and lanterns lining the sea wall. Every window of every house in the village glowed with candlelight. The people of Mousehole were calling their heroes home, but Tom would be returning alone.

The heavy wool dress and oil skin dragged her down. She kicked to keep at the surface, but her legs were tiring quickly. When another wave crashed down over her head everything went black.

***

Marie blinked and opened her eyes to daylight. She was cold. Chilled to the bone cold. She wasn't in a boat. She was lying on a shingle beach, her face pressed to the rounded pebbles. The last thing she recalled was her hand passing through Tom's as she'd fallen and it suddenly made sense. Of course she couldn't grab his hand. Tom hadn't saved his daughter and that could never change. She'd been shown something real. Not just shown but experienced something that had really happened centuries ago to Tom's daughter. Agatha. The vision gave the illusion that she was part of it, but it only went so far. She couldn't change the past.

She rolled to the side and awkwardly tried to sit up. A few little stones clung to her cheek and she brushed them away.

A whistle sounded down the beach and she turned. A young man hurried towards her. He wore a fluorescent vest.

Behind her, the sea wall loomed. She looked up and up to the top, where a line of curious faces peered down. Some of them were yelling and gesturing.

Footsteps crunched as people approached. The young man in the fluorescent vest reached her first and crouched beside her.

"Are you alright?" he asked.

Marie considered her reply. Was she? Something had happened last night that she couldn't explain and now she was here on the beach, with no idea how she got here. Her teeth started to chatter.

"Cold," she muttered. That was about all she was sure of right then.

A radio crackled. "We've found her, repeat, we've found her. All teams stand down."

A blanket appeared, and someone handed her a polystyrene cup full of hot, sweet tea. She looked up into the faces of all the strangers crowded around her and wondered how they had even known to look for her. And then, among the faces lined up along the sea wall, she saw the old woman she'd talked to the night before. The one whose granddaughter had held the fish lantern in the parade.

There were other faces she recognised too. A young lad who'd served her in the corner shop. The post woman. A man who'd walked his dog past her house on the morning she'd moved in and who'd waved to her every morning since.

Maybe she wasn't such an outsider after all. All the time she'd been worrying about being a fraud and these wonderful people had already accepted her as one of their own. They'd even noticed her disappearance and come searching. Like the lanterns calling Old Tom home all those years ago, they had rallied to protect their own.

Further along the sea wall, she spied a familiar bearded face. Old Tom put his hand to the brim of his hat, dipped his head and winked. And then he was gone. Faded away. But, somehow ever-present in that little Cornish village.

The Ancestors

Dolly Garland

Asha walked out of her apartment building, and turned towards the main road, which was busy even during the Diwali break with cars, mopeds, bicycles, pedestrians, occasional cows and dogs. A camel cart went past, carrying a load of vegetable sacks. The usual chaos continued, as people and animals went about their business, ignoring traffic lights and road signs.

Asha carefully avoided the cow pats, dog excrement, and muddy puddles. She followed a meandering route from the medium-rise buildings, full of the expanding middle-class, and onto a street of dilapidated council flats. She turned towards the first block and headed up the stairs, passing open doors protected with grilled metal lattices, to keep stray dogs out.

Her heartbeat boomed. Sweat trickled down her spine. Was she doing the right thing? What if it was just a dream? Asha firmly put aside the questions. She didn't need any more of them ... she needed answers. To avoid second-guessing herself, she focussed on her surroundings.

A woman was ironing a sari in one flat; in another a man sat on the bed, snipping his toenails; two half-naked boys wrestled and shouted. There was nothing to hide in lives that went on in unbroken cycles of duty, unfulfilled dreams and ambitions passed down as inheritance.

Asha knocked on number six. Dried, red kumkum handprints on the wall by the front door signalled a remnant of a religious occasion. She registered the details out of habit and forced herself to observe, remain calm, to feel normal.

A portly woman wearing a widow's white sari answered the door. She looked surprised, but smiled warmly. "Miss Asha!"

"I'm sorry to bother you on your day off, Saraswatiben," Asha said. She shouldn't have come. This was too dangerous a topic to risk gossip. And it was completely inappropriate. Saraswati was their servant. But she was also the only person Asha knew who might have some answers. In the past, Saraswati had often provided remedies for children falling ill from jealous eyes, or given tips to women who couldn't conceive. She knew rituals and mantras for appeasing gods, and once helped a woman recover from a disgruntled relative's curse.

Saraswati ushered her in. "Miss Asha, it's no bother. You are most welcome."

Asha stood in the middle of the one-room bedroom cum sitting room. Again, she deliberately focused on the ordinariness of her surroundings. A daybed took up one side of the room. Two chairs, a small TV, and a wooden table with idols of gods and prayer materials occupied the rest of the room.

"Miss Asha, what is it?" Saraswati's concerned tone forced Asha to focus.

Asha took a deep breath. There was nothing to gain by delay. She needed help. "I need your advice. It may sound absurd, and I'm probably wrong, but you must promise that you won't mention it to anyone."

Saraswati looked at her curiously, but nodded.

"Swear it on your son's life," Asha heard herself say. She needed whatever assurances she could get. If this turned out to be a mistake, she didn't want to end up as a neighbourhood lunatic.

She waited quietly, aware of Saraswati's hesitation. Not many people would casually swear on their child's life. Asha knew that Saraswati's pride and joy, and her only family, was her son. She made ends meet by cleaning houses so that he could study in Mumbai. It was this no-nonsense woman who Asha hoped knew about things most people wouldn't want anything to do with – such as dreams that felt real, and creatures who weren't human.

"Sit down, Miss Asha, and tell me what's on your mind."

Asha sat. "I've been having these... dreams. Except that I don't think they are dreams." Not knowing how to explain such a contradictory comment, Asha rolled up the sleeves of her kurta, baring the stark red scratches on her arms.

Saraswati gasped, and gently took hold of Asha's wrists to examine the marks.

"It's been happening for the last few days," Asha said, struggling to remain calm. She swallowed hard, rubbed her eyes to push away the welling tears. "The colours are so vivid. And I find myself by a river bank, near a banyan tree. Always in the same place. And these... creatures... surround me. I try to run away, but they never want to let me go." Asha shuddered at the memory of pale hands grasping her, scratching her.

"You say they are not humans?" Saraswati asked.

"They've human shape, but they are pale. Too pale. Their limbs are too long, and their bodies without hair."

Asha looked at Saraswati, wondering if the other woman believed her. Saraswati looked sincere. There was no scorn or obvious doubt on her face.

"How did you get away?" Saraswati asked.

"I don't know. I was struggling with them, and then I woke up in my bed."

"Miss Asha," Saraswati began in a too-gentle tone, "if you can get away by waking up, isn't it possible that you simply scratched yourself while you were having this nightmare?"

Asha clenched and unclenched her fists. Saraswati's doubts were justified. Anyone would have raised the same questions. In fact, most people – including her brother and sister-in-law – would have thought her crazy or drunk upon hearing this account.

"I also have scratches all down my back. I woke up this morning with muddy feet and dirty clothes. There was a thorn in my foot," Asha said, trying to sound matter-of-fact.

She almost expected Saraswati to not believe her. It occurred to her then why Saraswati may perhaps be indulging her.

"Saraswatiben," Asha said, "you don't need to pretend to believe me just because you work for us. My brother and sister-in-law don't know anything about this. I came to you because I thought you might be able to tell me what's going on. But if you think I'm imagining this, say so."

"I don't know what's true, Miss Asha. But I know you mean what you are saying," Saraswati said. "What else can you tell me about these creatures?"

"They seem soulless. Particularly their eyes. Looking into them is like staring into an abyss. But when I touch them, they are alive. I can feel their emotions, like they're trying to tell me something."

"What?"

"I don't know." Asha rubbed her forehead. It was frustrating that she'd no specific information to give. "They don't speak in words exactly. But I could feel them calling to me."

"Every time it's the same thing?"

"Last night was the longest and most intense. The first day, I just found myself on the river bank. I thought I saw something, and then I woke up in my room." Asha rose. The room was too tiny to pace, so she gazed out of the single window that looked into the living room of a similar flat across a narrow alley.

She turned back to Saraswati. "Yesterday, I was *there*. I could smell the river air and the animal faeces by the tree. My foot was tangled in thick vines when I fell over. And I felt them... their touch, their hot breath on my skin." Her voice broke. "I *want* it to be a dream. But I woke up in my bed, with a rip in my tunic. There was no mud on the floor, but there were stains on my bedsheets from my dirty feet."

"The creatures you describe, I'm not familiar with them," Saraswati said.

There was no contempt or disbelief in her tone, which relieved Asha.

"But many people in the olden days had an ability to see supernatural things, from the times when gods and demons lived amongst us," Saraswati continued. "Some of those bloodlines still survive. Perhaps you have a trace of magic in you."

"I'm twenty-two," Asha said. "I've never had such an experience before. If I'd magic, wouldn't I have felt this before?"

"Yes, perhaps. But I can't think of what else it may be. Did anyone in your family ever have such dreams?"

"No," Asha replied instantly. But in her mind, a door opened. A long-forgotten image of her dead father. She shoved it back where it came from. She shouldn't have come. She shouldn't have spoken about this to anyone. "I'm sorry I bothered you with this. It's silly. It's probably just a nightmare."

Asha started towards the door.

"Miss Asha, wait," Saraswati said.

Asha waited politely, hoping Saraswati wouldn't ask more questions.

"There is a woman, who looks after the Krishna temple by the old well. She used to be a friend of my granny's. Her name is Dayaben Bhatt. She may be able to help you."

"Thank you," Asha said, still feeling like a fool for having unburdened herself.

***

Asha washed the dirty sheets, mended her tunic, cleaned, cooked, read the newspaper, and finished the daily crossword. She did every chore she could think of. But though her hands remained busy, her mind refused to focus on the more mundane matters.

Magic? Was that really the answer? Asha didn't know what she'd expected to learn, but the possibility of her possessing some kind of magic hadn't even occurred to her.

What if it was true? What if people found out? She would be labelled a freak. Or worse, some kind of an evil witch. Her brother would probably disown her, or lock her up. No one would marry her. Her whole life would be ruined.

Realising that she was taking her anxiety out on the sheets she was trying to fold, Asha smoothed the creases and folded them properly.

Should she go to the woman Saraswati mentioned? What if these were just delusions? What if this woman, Dayaben, couldn't be trusted? She already regretted speaking to Saraswati. She didn't want to advertise her abnormality to other people. Unable to make up her mind, and unable to sit still, Asha left her flat again to buy groceries.

Just down the street from her apartment complex, vegetable merchants stood with their carts, advertising their wares by shouting. Asha carried on, heading towards the main market, a twenty-minute walk away.

The traffic continued in a steady flow. A group of boys were playing cricket on the street. Several kids were celebrating Diwali early, lighting sparklers. Young men sat or half-reclined over their motorbikes, idling away from their mothers' interfering eyes. They looked at Asha as she walked past. One of them whistled. Asha ignored them.

The vegetable market was crowded. As she made her selections, in a narrow gap between two buildings, she spotted a creature with long, white, hairless limbs. It jumped back into the shadows as soon as their eyes met.

Asha let out a startled cry, and dropped her groceries on the cart.

"What's wrong, madam? These are good onions. I give you a good price," said the merchant, an old man with rotten teeth and lips lined red with betel juice.

Asha stared at him blankly. She looked back again at where she'd seen the creature. Had it been there? But why here? In her world. While she was awake. Did that mean she was always going to see them?

"Madam, are you all right?" the merchant asked loudly.

Asha looked at him, tried to speak. Her throat was dry. She realised then that she was trembling. She couldn't' remember feeling so scared ever before.

She hurried away from the vegetable cart, confused by her ghostly vision.

A crippled beggar asked for money. On impulse, Asha put a ten rupee note in his bowl.

"May you be blessed with sons, beti," the beggar said, and called after her. "Beware of men with white skin and dead eyes."

Asha turned back. "What did you say?"

He gave her a toothless smile, and shrugged. "Don't remember."

"You said something about men with white skin and dead eyes."

The beggar shrugged again. "Don't know, beti. I say things, and I forget them."

The other beggars huddled around her. Two children approached her with outstretched hands. She had to leave. She should've known better. Paying one beggar was to invite them all. If she lingered, they'd surround her. But why had he spoken of the white men with dead eyes? Did he know something? Could he see them? Asha controlled an impulse to shake him.

For the last few days, she'd only seen these creatures after she fell asleep. But suddenly, after talking to Saraswati she'd seen one in daylight, and now there was someone else talking about them. What had changed?

"Tell me the truth, please," Asha implored the beggar. "Have you seen something? Dead eyes? Why did you say that?"

A beggar-child tugged at her dupatta.

The old beggar she'd given money to was smiling serenely, and shrugging.

"Money for an old man, madam?" He rattled his bowl. The ten rupee note she'd given him was gone already.

Asha pulled her dupatta back, and strode away. Questions rattled in her brain, and panic threatened to rise as bile. The children followed her for a while, then gave up. She didn't decrease her pace until she got home. She was perspiring – was it from the fast walk or was it from fear?

She called out a greeting when she got home, but there was no response, as expected. She didn't think her brother and sister-in-law would return before the late afternoon.

She washed her face with cold water and rinsed out her mouth. She put the groceries away, and, for lack of anything better to do, turned the TV on. As soon as the channel came into focus, she screamed, and dropped the remote.

The creatures were on the TV. Asha picked up the remote, and flicked the channel, but they were gone. She went back to the previous channel, and found just a regular soap opera.

"I'm going crazy."

Perhaps it was just fear. Her subconscious playing tricks.

Like it had played tricks on her father.

The memory came from nowhere. The door opened wider than it had in Saraswati's flat, and this time Asha wasn't able to shut it so quickly.

She remembered her father and mother arguing one Diwali, when Asha was seven years old. Her father gesturing at something her mother couldn't see. He'd then disappeared for hours, returning several hours later, dishevelled.

Several days later, for the first time, Asha had seen her father sobbing. It had shocked her. He was the head of the household. He was strong. Indian men didn't weep like women. But he was crying so hard, his entire body shook. She'd forgotten that. Like she'd forgotten so many things since her father's body was discovered in the Kankaria lake three years later, and her broken-hearted mother's death soon after.

Now she remembered. And as she did, another door opened in the deepest recess of her mind. Asha knew she needed to find the truth. Too many things had happened. Too many signs to prove this wasn't a dream.

She wanted to go and see Dayaben, but it was too big a risk. If people found out she was seeing strange creatures and ending up in places she'd no memory of, she would be ostracised. It wouldn't just affect her. Her family's respectability would be ruined. Her sister-in-law was about to have a baby. She couldn't do it to them. But if she didn't do anything, then she might actually go crazy.

***

The temple by the old well was reputed to be at least a hundred years old. Despite a fresh coat of paint, cracks in the structure showed its age. A small gate led to an open courtyard where there was a shoe stand, and several benches occupied by retired men and old women, who would sit there all day, gossiping about each other's families, dissing their daughters-in-law, praising grandchildren and passing the time of day.

The temple should've been busier than usual due to Diwali holidays, but there were newer, bigger temples in the area, and this one was largely ignored by those who only wanted to pray on special occasions or barter for favours.

Asha placed her shoes on the stand, and went into the temple. She prayed to Lord Krishna for answers, for this mystery to unravel, for her peace of mind to return. When she was done, she asked the priest, "Who is Dayaben Bhatt, Panditji?"

The priest pointed to an old woman with knitting needles. Asha thanked him, and cautiously approached the woman.

"Dayaben?"

The woman looked up, nodded.

"I wanted to speak with you. Saraswatiben Madhav said you might be able to help me."

"Oh?" The woman glanced at Asha for a moment, then ordered in the way elders were used to commanding. "Sit down."

Asha sat, wondered where to start so that it wouldn't make her sound crazy, and realised there was no such way. So she told Dayaben about her dreams, and about the possibility that her father might also have been able to see these creatures.

Dayabaen listened, occasionally making eye contact. When Asha finished, she asked, "Do you know about Gandharvas?"

"I know of them. From mythology," Asha said. The last time she'd heard about them was from Mahabharata. They were demigods, guardians of nature. Immensely beautiful in appearance, they also made music that could make gods swoon.

"The creatures you are seeing are the lost Gandharvas."

"That's ridiculous," Asha said. "Gandharvas aren't demonic spirits with dead eyes."

"They aren't demonic. They are ghosts. A remnant of what they used to be."

Asha covered her face with her hands. This was too much. Perhaps Gandharvas had existed when gods supposedly walked the earth. But how could these creatures be those demigods? They weren't majestic, or godlike.

But Dayaben's conviction seemed stronger than Asha's doubts, so Asha asked, "What do they want from me?"

Because they did want something, Asha realised. If they wanted to kill her, or brutally attack her, they could've done that the first time. Each time it had felt more intense, because each time they'd been more insistent on communicating with her. But she'd been too afraid to notice.

"They want to go home. They are trapped here."

"Can you see them too?"

"No."

"Then how do you know?"

"My sister could see them. I've known about them all my life."

"Did she help them?"

Dayaben smiled, sadly. "She wasn't strong enough." She scrutinised Asha with brown eyes framed by wrinkles. "You're stronger. I think you can help them."

"Help them how?"

"Ask them."

***

The last thing Asha remembered was her eyelids drooping, then waking up near the river. Close to a banyan tree. Her instincts screamed for her to run, but she stayed still, fists clenched at her side.

They moved towards her. She noticed, for the first time, that they were gliding rather than walking. Their faces were expressionless. Yet, she felt their eagerness. As if they could already sense the change in her. That she was willing to communicate.

They were soon near her, close. Too close. And then they stopped.

Asha remained rooted to the spot, as firm as the ancient tree she sat beneath. She was still scared. Still unsure of what this meant, and where it might lead. But she managed to speak, though her voice rasped. "What do you want from me?"

One of the creatures reached out to touch her. Asha recoiled, and the hand stopped.

Asha stopped moving, and the Gandharva reached out again.

Its hand touched her forehead, and there was an explosion in her skull. Asha closed her eyes, clenched her teeth. In her mind, there was brightness, music, and more beauty than she could have imagined. Forests and rivers, mountains and streams, snow and sunlight. The vibrancy of colours made her feel like she was looking through sharper, younger eyes. Or older. Eyes that could see time in its perpetuity.

Just as Asha was starting to relax, new images flickered in her mind. They were vivid too, but the trees were yellow and brown; the rivers were muddy and full of corpses; plants were dying, mountains eroding, and the streams dry; the music which had been completely at harmony with nature, now felt dissonant, becoming loud and aggressive.

The scene changed again, and the land transformed into buildings. In those dead trees and mountains, amongst the muddy rivers and dried-up streams, there were watchful spirits with their instruments. But the music which had once sustained them now brought them pain, and added to the disharmony all around them.

The discord increased. The music grew louder, until it was nothing but noise. Asha pressed her hands over her ears, but couldn't make it stop. The odd notes and jarring tunes sent painful pulsations through her brain.

"Stop!"

The vivid colours hurt her eyes, even though she'd clenched them shut. Her head and her ears ached from the noise. The past, not just her past but that of an entire race, intruded on her present; the visceral reaction from it had her whimpering. Asha felt herself falling, curling up on the leaf-strewn, dirt-caked riverbank.

The sound shook her nerves as if someone was using them as guitar strings, but with no musical skills or delicacy for handling an instrument. So much noise, increasing in tempo. Harder and harder. And the pain increased with it.

"Stop. Please." Asha thrashed on the ground.

The sounds stopped. The deadness in her mind disappeared. There were echoes still, but they were fading. She opened her eyes. The Gadharvas were still looking at her, but none of them were touching her.

"Why did you do that?" she asked.

They didn't answer.

One of them reached out again.

"No." Asha scooted away. She couldn't bear that noise again, or those images.

She got to her feet. "I don't know what you want. You can't keep doing this to me. I've never done anything to harm you."

She was angry at herself for believing those old hags, Saraswati and Dayaben. These creatures weren't benign. They were evil.

She needed to get out. Asha slapped her cheeks, willing herself to wake up. But she was still there, and they were crowding her again.

One of them held up his its hands in a placating gesture. Asha stopped moving.

"Don't touch me again. It hurts." She wasn't sure if they understood her. The creatures, all of them at once, pointed behind her. Towards the tree. Slowly, she turned.

And screamed.

Her father, older and weaker than in her memory, but unmistakably him, leaned against the tree trunk as if he couldn't support his own weight.

"Papa!"

Asha ran towards him. She reached out a hesitant hand, touched his shoulder, and found flesh. He was no illusion.

She hugged him.

"Papa. How's this possible? What happened to you? Where've you been?"

He said nothing, and didn't return the embrace.

Asha pulled back, confused. She looked into his brown eyes, and froze.

They were no longer brown. They were black, like the creatures.

"Papa?"

He turned his head, and something flickered in his eyes. A fleck of brown returned.

He reached out, touched her cheek.

Asha covered his palm with hers, tears burning her eyes. He pressed his hand further into her skin, and she felt another flash of memories swimming in her head.

She saw him as she remembered him; young, with a slight paunch. Laughing, fighting with her mother, coming home from work, lifting her up. Memories. Then she saw him here in the same spot. All those years ago, as confused as she'd been the first time.

The creatures were crowding him just as they crowded her.

Asha jumped back from her father. "Is this what they will do to me? Make me like this?"

Her father shook his head, reached out his hand again.

Tentatively, Asha took it.

More memories. His repeat visits to the creatures, every Diwali. The tone of the meetings changed, as he stopped being afraid of them. He sat amongst them, holding hands with the creatures, his expression changing from fear and pain to serenity as he travelled through their memories.

"Why are you showing me this?" Asha asked.

He placed both his hands on her temples, and touched her forehead with his. Instead of images, as she'd been expecting, she heard his thoughts.

Hello, beti.

"Papa? Is that really you?" Asha spoke out loud. She assumed he could hear her thoughts if she could hear his, but she'd no control over her thoughts. Speaking words out loud gave them a structure. A structure she so desperately wanted in this non-reality.

Yes. I can't do this for long, so you must pay attention.

"You are alive?"

Not quite, Asha. You must listen to me. I'm stuck. In limbo. With them.

"They did this to you?"

They didn't know this would happen. They only wanted my help. They have been here too long.

"Are they Gandharvas?"

She felt his surprise. And pride.

You know more already than I ever did. Their world is long gone. The ones who saw it coming left the earth. But the others didn't believe things would change so much. They were blinded by their magic, and their power. Now, they are stuck. Decaying but not dying.

"What can I do?"

You can free them, and me.

"Why did they attack me then, if they are kin?"

They didn't mean to, beti. They were trying to talk to you, but until you were willing to listen, the connection could not be formed. Each time you left, there was a risk you might never return. They were scared of losing their chance yet again.

Asha considered that. They'd seemed rather desperate. And this time, from the beginning, they'd done nothing that seemed like they were going to attack her. Because they'd sensed they could now talk to her. As they had, to her father.

She wished she could just hold on to him. All the years of being without a father. Could she have him back? Or would she become like him?

"Papa, what if I get stuck too, like you did?"

You won't. You are stronger than me, and I had plenty of time to figure this out. But you must do exactly as I say.

"Okay."

You need to let them connect with you. They will merge with you.

"Possess me?"

Become a part of you. You've Gandharva blood in you, beti. So do I. That's why we can see them.

"But I only started seeing them recently."

On Diwali.

"How do you know?"

The auspiciousness of Diwali, festivities and prayers, just before the new moon comes, gives them more strength. They are able to harness their combined powers to reach out to one of us. For them to be free, their highest chances of success are at Diwali. But it doesn't mean you wouldn't have seen them at other times. I did.

More memories, forgotten or buried, flooded back. She hadn't imagined it in the market. There had been other times too. Throughout her childhood. The reason why she used to be scared of going out alone to play. The reason why she'd avoided parks and green spaces. The reason why at Diwali, she thought she'd heard voices. It all made sense now, slotted into her mind like pieces of a puzzle.

"Would I still be me, Papa? What if they control me?"

They won't. They will give you their memories, their life-force. Eventually they will fade away, leaving a part of them in you.

"Why can't they fade now?"

They are trapped ghosts. They can't die. They need to shed these half-bodies, so their souls can be free. They've decayed far too much to be able to do it alone.

"What about you? Will you become a part of me too?"

Only for a few moments. I'm not strong enough to survive long.

"What if you remain here? I can come and visit."

No beti. The longer I stay, the more I will decay too.

"Papa, I don't want to lose you again."

Dead do not belong here, Asha. You will never lose me. I'm always in your heart, and now I'll be a part of these memories too.

Asha wiped her tears. She'd lost her father long ago, but at least this time she could say goodbye. She hugged him. Holding onto the wraithlike body, pretending he was what she remembered. He kissed her forehead.

Asha pulled back. She would do this for him. She would free him, and the people he'd sacrificed his life for.

"What must I do?"

Let them connect with you. Don't resist.

Asha turned to the Gandharva. Her ancestors. She sat down, and they formed a close circle around her, holding hands. She felt them starting to connect. Her instinct was to resist, but she lowered her guard as her father's soothing presence encouraged her. He was the first to transfer. She felt him, as if he'd walked through a door in her mind.

The others followed, one by one. As more and more of them made their way into her mind, she was overwhelmed. A cacophony of voices and consciousness invaded her. She couldn't distinguish herself from them, couldn't separate her thoughts and memories from theirs. Her head felt full to bursting. Her limbs were getting far too many conflicting signals from her brain. It felt like a bomb had exploded in her head, and her thoughts were flying debris.

***

Asha woke to the sound of insistent knocking. She remembered locking her bedroom door, and then other memories flooded in. She sat up, and placed her head in her hands as the blood rushed.

"Asha, are you awake?" It was her sister-in-law.

"Yes. I'll be out soon."

"Are you all right? Are you sick?"

"No... no, I just overslept."

"Okay, if you are sure."

When her sister-in-law had gone, Asha checked her appearance in the mirror. She was dirty again. Her sheets and clothes were muddy. But there were no scratches or any other marks on her.

Her head felt normal. It felt like her.

Had it happened? Had they all merged into her? Surely she would have been able to sense it. Maybe the pain she felt when they tried it meant she had failed. Meant she couldn't handle it.

Asha felt a strange sense of loss. If she'd failed, they were still stuck. Would they try again? Would they insist she visit them? How long would this go on for? And her father? What about him? She didn't want him decaying further.

She changed the bedsheets, and hurried to the bathroom, covering most of her body with the bulk of a towel and an armful of fresh clothing.

When she was out of the shower, she went to the balcony to hang her towel. Her gaze landed on the garden below. The blooming marigolds were the most vibrant golds and yellows she'd ever seen, and the blades of grass contained so many hues of green that Asha wondered why she'd never noticed it before.

She remembered when the grass was abundant and perpetually lush, and when marigolds were the size of her palm. She remembered the rich, fertile land and the gardens when gods roamed the earth. The land that was no less beautiful than heaven.

These memories, so vivid, but not her own, made her realise all that had been lost. Not just in the land and in the nature's beauty, but the loss of an entire race and the world they had known.

The Gandharvas had witnessed the changing world, and the decay of their own race. They'd become a myth. And now, all that would remain of them were the memories contained within her. For the duration of her life span. A mere blink of an eye from their perspective.

The sadness was overpowering. As Asha looked at the vista that was so familiar, she was aware of the changes within her; aware that she would never be able to look at the world in the same way again.

"I'll pass down this knowledge," she said out loud. "In whatever way I can. Your race won't be forgotten. I promise."

Then, a whisper in her mind.

Goodbye, beti.

"Goodbye, papa."

Asha wiped her tears, and stood for a while longer, gazing out at the world that was her own, and the world of her ancestors.

THE RAVEN'S DEATH
by Ian McConaghy
Westminster Hall Burial Grounds, Baltimore, Maryland, USA.
When I look back, my memory is unreliable. I recall Henry Herring, instructing me to arrange my cousin's funeral.
In a state of shock following his sudden death, I felt detached and struggled to order my thoughts.
I now feel great sorrow that we did not adequately commemorate his passing, on that day, 8th October 1849.
GENTLEMEN, WOULD YOU BE KIND ENOUGH TO ASSIST?
IT WOULD BE AN HONOUR, SIR.
COME ALONG, GENTLEMEN. I HAVE ANOTHER SERVICE TO ATTEND.
WE ARE GATHERED HERE TODAY TO BURY THE WRITER AND POET...
EDGAR ALLAN POE
The Reverend WTD Clemm was invited to carry out the service. Sadly, so few attended that he decided not to waste time on a sermon. He rushed away, leaving our sorry little group staring uncomfortably across the gaping grave. (from Neilson Poe's Journal)

SUCH A TRAGIC FAMILY. THOSE POOR WOMEN!
ELIZA
FRANCES
Our cousin, Elizabeth Herring, recounted the deaths which followed Edgar throughout his short life. She placed flowers upon the grave and then left, to pass on the news of his death.
AND VIRGINIA
AND NOW , DEAR, DEAR EDGAR
DR MORAN, WHAT HAPPENED IN EDGAR'S LAST DAYS?
HE ARRIVED INCOHERENT AND DELIRIOUS, MR SNODGRASS.
DURING THE NIGHT, HE STARTED SHOUTING AT THE WALLS.
Joseph Evans Snodgrass, a publisher and friend of Edgar's,came to pay his last respects. He tried to elicit information from Dr Moran, resident physician at Washington College Hospital.

And the Raven, never flitting, still is sitting, still is sitting
On the pallid bust of Pallas just above my chamber door;
And his eyes have all the seeming of a demon's that is dreaming,
And the lamp-light o'er him streaming throws his shadow on the floor;
And my soul from out that shadow that lies floating on the floor
Shall be lifted- nevermore!
Nevermore
Nevermore
NEVERMORE!
BY SUNDAY MORNING, HE WAS QUIET AND REGAINED CONSCIOUSNESS
YOU WILL SOON BE IN THE COMPANY OF FRIENDS!
THE BEST THING A FRIEND MIGHT DO IS BLOW MY BRAINS OUT!
LORD HELP MY POOR SOUL!
THOSE WERE HIS LAST WORDS.
Dr Moran informed us that Edgar had been unconscious. His stupor was then succeeded by 'tremor of the limbs' as well as delirium with 'constant talking and vacant converse with spectral and imaginary objects on the walls'. What had been going through his mind in those last few hours of his life?

In the cab taking us to Ryan's Tavern, despite Henry being brusque and impatient, Joseph Clarke and Zacharias Lee shared fond memories of their friend, Edgar.

Beset by drink problems, Edgar's father had left his wife with three young children so Henry and Snodgrass both thought drink had caused Edgar's death. After all, we did find him lying unconscious in Ryan's Tavern. It was Dr Moran's contention, however, that Edgar was not drunk. What had actually killed him?

Poor health had plagued the Poe family. Eliza, Frances and Virginia had all died of tuberculosis. Edgar himself had once suffered from cholera and had a fever in the days before he left Richmond. He tried to live from his writing. Often poor, he was forced to write begging letters, which eventually destroyed his relationship with his foster father, John Allan.

THIS IS WHERE WE FOUND EDGAR.
SNODGRASS HAD BOOKED HIM A ROOM AT THE TAVERN...
BUT WE TOOK HIM STRAIGHT TO THE HOSPITAL INSTEAD.
Edgar left Richmond on 27th September 1849, bound for Baltimore, the first stop on his way to New York, where he had been commissioned to edit a book of poetry. Sadly, he didn't get that far. I never received a satisfactory answer to what happened between the time he embarked and when we found him, unconscious in Ryan's Tavern.
HUFF! EDGAR HAD NO SELF-CONTROL
SO, WHAT DO YOU THINK HAPPENED?

BONJOUR MESSIEURS. MAY I JOIN YOU?
HOW MAY WE HELP YOU?
I HAVE RECENTLY WORKED WITH MONSIEUR POE.
HE WAS RESEARCHING HIS NEW BOOK 'MY HEART LAID BARE'...
ARE YOU A WRITER, SIR?
NON MONSIEUR. I AM A RATIOCINATOR:
A LOGICAL THINKER.
WILL THAT HELP EXPLAIN EDGAR'S MISSING DAYS?
FIRST WE MUST GATHER THE FACTS
HUFF! IT'S A MYSTERY. FIVE DAYS! THEN WE FIND HIM IN SOMEONE ELSE'S CLOTHES.
I don't know if it was the effect of alcohol as we toasted Edgar farewell, the emotional turmoil of the occasion or the unsettling words of the French gentleman but something conjured a most extraordinary vision in my mind.

SIR, WE HAVE NO INFORMATION!
I AM CERTAIN THAT EDGAR HAS LEFT US A CLUE
PERHAPS THIS WALKING CANE?
OH.. AND WE FOUND A KEY IN HIS POCKET?
ZACHARIAS, PULL THE HANDLE FROM THE CANE.
MY GOD! IT'S A SWORD.
YOU WILL NEED TO FIND EDGAR'S TRUNK
THIS KEY WILL OPEN IT
PLACE THE SWORD INSIDE AND THEN KEY IN THE CODE.
NEILSON, LOOK AT THE KEY.
EXAMINE THEM BOTH CLOSELY.
CLICK!
CLICK!
CLICK!
CLUNK!
IT WILL RELEASE A HIDDEN COMPARTMENT.
AND REVEAL A MANUSCRIPT
MESSIEURS, I MUST NOW DEPART.
BUT SIR. WHAT IS YOUR NAME?
C. AUGUSTE DUPIN.
AU REVOIR.
Distracted, examining the intricate markings upon the sword, we hardly noticed Dupin leave and Snodgrass arrive. Uncle Henry had the forethought to obtain the gentleman's name.

WHO WAS THAT MAN YOU WERE TALKING TO?
A FOREIGN GENTLEMAN BY THE NAME OF DUPIN.
THAT..THAT CANNOT BE...
I PUBLISHED A STORY BY EDGAR CALLED THE MYSTERY OF MARIE ROGET.
IT WAS SOLVED BY C. AUGUSTE DUPIN.
EDGAR WAS A MASTER OF THE HOAX. HAS HE PLAYED ONE MORE, ZACHARIAS?
WE MUST FIND THE TRUNK, JOSEPH, AND DECRYPT HIS MESSAGE.
Snodgrass was startled by the revelation. How could the man be a character from Poe's novel? Months later, Zacharias found the trunk in Richmond. Following Dupin's instructions he retrieved the so-called manuscript. It was in code and took weeks to decipher. Alas, it was incomprehensible but for a few moments of lucidity. In the end, our conclusion was that these were the musings of a mad man.

My thoughts have again returned to that strange meeting in the Tavern. We never saw that man again. Who was he? Could he be some itinerant actor, engaged by Edgar, to provoke our feelings at this sad time? Perhaps we had imagined him. Had we summoned a ghost in our highly emotional state? Was Poe trying to communicate with us, as his soul departed this world?
We never again discussed Dupin. Perhaps we feared that the madness which seemed to descend upon Edgar in those last few days would eventually touch us all. Perhaps it already has.
Neilson Poe, 1849

Empty Chairs

M E Rodman

Gillian lifted the plate out of the soapy dishwater and defiantly put it on the draining board, without rinsing. She could see Maureen behind her, though in the blurred reflection of the night-dark kitchen window, she couldn't make out her mother-in-law's features.

She didn't need to.

She could feel the woman's disapproval drilling into her spine. Staring into the window, Gillian allowed herself a small, petty smile before picking up the next plate. By the time she had finished, Maureen was gone.

This time of year, it was dark by five. Gillian, having twice cleaned plates dusty from being stored in the cupboard since last year, turned to the cooker and the makings of dinner.

It had been years ago, in that little flat above the takeaway, that Steve told her about the Pearce family tradition. Gillian had always thought it odd and more than a little tasteless. But then, Halloween was her least favourite time of the year. The sweets were sickening, the decorations tacky and the dressing up was childish – even for the children.

"Obviously the dead don't really visit," Steve had said earnestly, "but it's comforting somehow, being able to think of them like that."

She loved Steve and it made him happy, so she had dutifully laid that extra plate for dinner every Halloween, honouring dead relatives that Steve had never even met.

Then Steve's parents had come to live with them. Maureen could no longer manage stairs, so Steve built a little annexe onto the side of the house. They had their own bedroom, living room, kitchen and toilet. And yet, somehow, they always ended up in the main house.

Steve's father, Frank, was always cracking bad jokes and forever smoking cheap cigarettes, though everyone told him they were dangerous for Natalie because of her asthma ... Maureen never said much. But the way she watched Gillian, her blue-rinse head tilted to one side, said just how inadequate she found her daughter-in-law to be. Sometimes Gillian's jaw ached from clenching her teeth.

When Maureen finally succumbed to a bad chill that settled on her chest, it was something of a relief. Though, of course, Gillian would never say that.

Maureen died in June and things had settled down by the time Halloween rolled around. Everyone was sad, naturally, especially Frank, but time was a great healer. In the light of their loss, Gillian had questioned the tastefulness of continuing the tradition but Steve was adamant.

"Halloween was Mum's favourite time of year. She'd have wanted us to."

So dutifully, Gillian had dished up the extra plate, meat, veg and potatoes and placed it before the empty chair.

It was a subdued meal.

The food sat there while they ate, the gravy congealing, the roast going cold. Such a waste; Gillian had spent an hour piping those potatoes into florets. No one mentioned it but the empty chair kept catching their eyes.

It was a relief to clear the table.

Gillian wasn't sure how long it was before she realised that Maureen had come back. It wasn't as if Gillian could see her. It was more of a feeling, the sensation of eyes digging into the back of her head. An impression of disapproval as Gillian scrubbed the sink or bleached the front doorstep.

Occasionally she caught a glimpse out of the corner of her eye or on shiny surfaces. But they never lasted long.

Gillian hoped that the next Halloween would take Maureen away. But it didn't. She stayed, a silent presence, purposefully making no comment on Gillian's pumpkin and pistachio roulade.

By the second anniversary of Maureen's death, Frank was showing signs of increasing decrepitude. He never left the house. Instead he spent his days in an armchair in the living room, a plaid blanket over his knees, watching old black and white movies.

He started talking to himself, mumbling away in an awkward fashion that Gillian found unnerving. His fixture in the living room made it difficult for Gillian to shampoo the carpet or wash the walls and the room became increasingly grubby.

Sometimes Gillian would come in, to do the evening vacuuming, to find both Steve and Natalie sitting on the couch, with Frank in his chair. They would be laughing together over some puerile comedy show or family-friendly movie – Natalie shamelessly neglecting her homework. The chair on the far side of the room always bore the shadow of Maureen as if they were encouraging her, though Gillian was sure they did not see her at all. Gillian would go and scrub the toilets until the show was over and she could get at the carpet.

About a year after Maureen's passing she finally, with gentle firmness, persuaded Frank to give up smoking. Steve had protested. "Dad was getting really good at going outside," he said.

But Gillian reminded him that it was better for Frank's health in the end. Not to mention Natalie's asthma *and* the soft furnishings.

She still found the odd packet tucked down the side of the armchair. She crumpled each one determinedly and put them in the bin.

***

Frank passed away in December, so it was almost a year before Gillian had to make any fateful decisions. It was a year in which Maureen seemed more pervasive than ever. Gillian could sense her inspecting the corners of the room for cobwebs and investigating plug holes for hair.

The washing up, sat soapy on the draining board, took on an ominous air.

Gillian knew it was ridiculous; the woman was dead after all. But she couldn't seem to help it.

She cleaned until the house was spotless. Scrubbed and polished the surfaces to a high shine. There was not a table leg out of place or a smudge to be found anywhere. The air smelt of lemon and mint, and sometimes, despite Gillian's best efforts, of Rose of Attar, Maureen's favourite perfume.

The cleaning reached such a level that even Steve noticed.

"Blimey!" He joked when he came downstairs for a glass of milk at two in the morning to find Gillian scrubbing the kitchen floor. "Are you sure you're not channelling my mother?"

Gillian smiled weakly, she was far better at keeping house than Maureen had ever been.

Eventually the days cooled, September faded into October, and it was Halloween again. Natalie came back from a trip to the shops after school with a witch costume, three carrier bags full of sweets and a very large pumpkin. Gillian didn't say anything. Steve helped Natalie carve it.

There would be just the three of them for dinner. The house had grown quiet over the last year. It seemed too big and empty. Gillian still got a shock when she walked into the living room to find it deserted, the TV silent in the corner. Frank's blanket folded on the chair where he used to sit.

She was stirring the gravy on the stove, the plates drying on the rack behind her, when Natalie walked in.

"Can I help?" she asked.

There were shadows under her eyes. She missed her granddad still, after all this time.

Gillian summoned a smile.

"Of course you can, dear. Why don't you cut up the carrots, batons, not rounds."

She picked up the plates and went into the dining room. Standing before the table she counted out the plates in her arms. One, two, three.

Three.

She hesitated. There were three living people in her family. She didn't have to feed the dead. What if the chairs and the food were an invitation? What if this was all her fault? Was Maureen here because she had encouraged her? If she never laid the extra plate would the dead be un-invited?

It was very tempting.

No more watching eyes. No more knowing disapproval.

Then she thought of Steve and Natalie. It gave them comfort to see those untouched plates, those empty chairs. Steve had lost his father, Natalie, her grandad, they were looking forward to this.

Gillian sighed.

She laid down the plates, all five of them, with defiant hands.

At dinner her family was in a good mood. They laughed and chatted and told a whole load of Frank's terrible jokes. They even approved of the pumpkin and pineapple jelly Gillian served for the dessert. She felt satisfied just seeing their faces.

Afterwards, Natalie dragged Steve off to watch *Hocus Pocus* in the living room. Gillian sat looking at the remains. She wasn't sure if Maureen was there; she couldn't sense her. It crossed Gillian's mind that maybe Maureen had just been waiting for Frank. Perhaps they had moved on together. The thought made her step lighter as she walked around the table.

After all, who had ever heard of the dead actually coming to Halloween dinner, it was ridiculous.

She glanced at the empty chairs as she gathered up the untouched plates. The lamb had gone a disturbing sort of grey and the carrots were decidedly limp. The room was quiet, the hum of the television muted by distance.

Then as Gillian turned towards the kitchen, plates in hand, she smelt it. Rose of Attar mixed with cigarette smoke. It filled the room, beating back the lemon and mint freshness.

She turned back to the empty chairs, her fingers tightening on the plates. They were there.

Gillian turned to the kitchen, plates in hand. She headed straight for the sink. She did not look back, she did not need to, the image was clear in her memory. Across the table on those empty chairs were the wrinkled and grey-haired figures of her in-laws. They rested at ease with no sign of ever moving. There was a twinkle in their bright, watching eyes.

Your Honest, Sonsie Face

Ken Shinn

The Burns Night feast had been extremely satisfying. I'd felt honoured when the local laird, Torcail McCrimmon, had sent me the invitation, especially since I was a southern-dwelling Sassenach of fairly short acquaintance. His bank account was held with our establishment, and last year I'd helped him deal with a tricky investment problem. We'd met at his mansion three or four times, and I'd sorted the whole situation out and even advised him on further financial alleys that he might wish to pursue. In our first meeting, he'd been cautious and business-like, but by the last few meetings, he had become more cordial, though still far from a close friend. He had thanked me at the end of our last meeting, and smiled slyly, saying that he'd have to find a way of repaying his debt to me some day.

Well, he'd found it, and I had to admit that I'd had a lot of fun, and even managed not to embarrass myself in a kilt too much. There'd been much vigorous flinging, high wit and low jokes, a good deal of lively banter, and exuberant bagpipes, and I'd loved it all. But most of all, I now had an unexpected love of haggis.

Like many people, I found the idea of haggis distinctly revolting. Seasoned oats and innards, served up in a stomach? I'd taken several tumblers of the laird's excellent whiskey to brace myself for eating the thing. However, the air of fond ceremony as the great dish was borne to the table, the recitation of the traditional address, and the almost reverent slicing-open of the haggis itself demanded my respect, and the gush of savoury steam that burst forth along with the rich, dark innards definitely smelled very good. I found my mouth watering as the plates were filled and passed around the long table, heaped high with tatties, neeps – and the haggis itself.

There was one odd thing about the whole ritual, however. Before those at the table were served, Torcail rose from his seat, bearing a heavily-laden platter in one hand, and a decanter of whiskey in the other. He carried these solemnly to a spot on the far wall, where an intricately-stitched rug had been placed in anticipation, precisely beneath an odd, discoloured patch on the wall itself.

The patch had a yellow-brown hue. It could have been damp rot in the walls, it could have been a stain caused by generations of tobacco, but it seemed unremarkable from where I sat. Certainly not singular enough to explain why the laird arranged his burden on the rug, before bowing respectfully low and then returning to the head of the table. No one else, apart from me, seemed surprised by this – it seemed to be a tradition.

That aside, the haggis was downright delicious. My queasy preconceptions were unfounded. I was sure that this wasn't simply down to the anaesthetic properties of the whiskey and I was glad to accept a second serving. The feasting, dancing and general revelry that ensued left me replete, half-cut, and happily exhausted: but that strange, ceremonial moment nagged at the back of my mind. As the night drew to a close, and the other guests departed to their homes, I decided to question the laird about it.

As he bade a fond farewell to the last stragglers, I picked up my glass, topped it up, and strolled over to the patch on the wall. From my closer view, I could make out its details more clearly. It was about the size of my head, and, as I leant nearer, an odd, giddy sensation swept over me.

As a child, I'd been upset by the floral wallpaper in my bedroom, and my long-suffering parents eventually replaced it with a more acceptable design of rockets and astronauts. What had disturbed me so much was that, viewed from just the right angle, there were faces staring back at me. Misshapen, threatening faces.

The patch on the wall looked very like a man's face, smiling with what looked like contented triumph. The face of someone who'd won some important, personal victory, the brows lowered over half-closed eyes and that wide, upturned mouth. It looked like it knew something that I didn't. My childhood fear surged up in me again, but whiskey and adulthood swept it firmly away. I remained gazing at it in fascination.

"Ah, I see that you've noticed Auld Fergus," said a cheery voice behind me, causing me to start. Mercifully, I didn't spill my drink. "Our very own Turin Shroud, isn't he?" I turned to see the laird, his boyish face grinning and slightly flushed with whiskey. His tone grew solemn. "And here's to him. Now, and always." He raised his glass to the patch. I realised that he was entirely serious, and hesitantly raised my own.

He could have been talking to himself. "Our best to you, Auld Fergus. You are not forgotten." He took a long swallow from his drink. I joined him in the gesture.

As he held his gaze on the face for a moment longer, I decided to ask. "Torcail, pardon my ignorance – but who is Auld Fergus, and why is he so important to you?"

He looked at me thoughtfully. "That, as people say, is an interesting story. I'll tell you if you want, but you might not believe me. Although that doesn't really matter – because I believe it. And so does everyone else in this village."

Whiskey made me voluble.

"Well, the night is dark, the fire is bright, and the drink is good. What better way to tell a tale?"

The laird smiled, though his eyes remained haunted. "Very well, Peter. Let's make ourselves comfortable." I picked up a fresh decanter and followed him into the lounge. We settled ourselves comfortably in ancient, overstuffed armchairs before the blazing logs in the hearth and refreshed our drinks.

He gathered his thoughts for a few moments.

"Peter, the tale of Auld Fergus McNae and Donald McCrimmon is an old one, but not ancient. It all happened a couple of centuries ago. It's a story of many things – innocence, idealism, rivalry, murder, and retribution. Unnatural retribution."

"And ghoulies and ghosties and long-leggedy beasties and things that go bump in the night?"

"Peter, shut up and listen, will you?"

His reproof was mild, but there was a definite hardness to his voice as well. I knew that the sudden fresh flush in my cheeks wasn't just down to the drink.

"Sorry," I muttered. "Please go on."

"It all began with the Industrial Revolution. Donald was my direct ancestor, and himself the laird in his day. By the late 1800s, our family had established themselves in this village, not only as lairds, but as prominent businessmen – and we made our fortune in meat. For centuries, the McCrimmons have been the most renowned butchers in the country, among those who know the value of good food. Donald was no exception, and, when the Revolution came, he was quick to realise the benefits that he could reap. He installed all sorts of wonderful new machinery in his factory – automated knives, steam hoses, and his pride and joy, an enormous mincing machine capable of turning an entire carcass into finely-chopped meat in a matter of moments.

"Donald was an odd fellow. On the one hand, a loving husband and father, and a successful dealer and employer, as well as a man known to be well able of holding his drink in the local pubs, and buying his rounds. On the other... well, he had something of a temper, capable of rages that matched his huge frame in size and power – and, though he paid his workers well, he cared little for their wellbeing.

"There were a lot of accidents and injuries on the slaughterhouse floor, as the new machines presented more problems for men unskilled in their use. Nobody was killed, but scars were left, fingers were partially or wholly removed... and, eventually, an unlucky crewman named Gordon Sutherland had his right arm caught in that mincing machine. It was shorn clear from his body before anybody could rescue him. Thanks to his own sheer bloody-mindedness and swift help from his fellow workers, his life was saved, but he was invalided and spent the rest of his days a crippled and embittered loner.

"It didn't matter how well the laird paid. The workers were getting more and more discontented with the safety conditions in the place. But they didn't have a figurehead, a good man that they could rally behind. At least, until Fergus McNae started work in the laird's factory.

"We call him Auld Fergus out of... affectionate respect. And also because this was all centuries ago. But the man himself was young, barely in his twenties, and fresh from a first term at the University of Edinburgh in the autumn of 1880 that had infected him with a severe case of socialism. He came home that winter and took up a temporary job with Donald, glad of the pay, but it was only days before he saw the horrors of the slaughterhouse floor for himself. What shocked him most, though, was that his fellow workers seemed prepared to accept their lot – at least at first. The more that he spoke with them, the more he became convinced that their justified fears and resentments could bring a weight of opinion to bear on the laird and result in a change for the better.

"So he arranged to meet the laird in his office. The man was initially friendly, offering him a large single malt from the decanter on his desk, and listened with apparent patience and interest as Fergus made his case. As the minutes passed, the younger man realised that he was being treated with amused contempt, which made him all the more determined to be heard. His voice grew loud enough to be heard through the heavy door, but this only served to escalate Donald's contempt into overt, roaring anger.

"Shortly afterward, a clear, furious yell was heard. 'Get out of my office, you stupid little prick, back to work, *and never dare bring this sort of fucking nonsense to me again!'*

"Fergus closed the office door behind him with careful quiet. He was shaking with fear and anger. Once he'd composed himself, he went to speak quietly with his closest friends among the other workers. An agreement was reached, and the next day they conversed in turn with some of their fellows. A plan was being laid, starting with a meeting in the back room of one of the village inns that night.

"The following morning, the laird took his customary stroll of the factory floor. He realised that something wasn't right, and the problem became quickly apparent. While work was progressing, a lot of the machines stood idle, most obviously the mincer, whose great blades had been silenced. That meant output down, and a consequent reduction of profit. Donald's ensuing shout echoed around the whole building. 'Who's turned the bloody machines off? Get them started again right now, or I'll dock all of your wages!'

"It was then that he saw the group of men walking towards him, and Fergus was leading them. As they halted, the young man addressed the laird directly. 'That isn't going to happen, Donald. Not until you do something about the conditions in this place. We've had enough of the bloodshed. Oh, we'll be happy to work again – once you've done your part, and made it safer. If you don't – then we strike.'

"Fergus, the laird realised with shock, had a certain authority to him. While his voice was quiet, it was absolutely cold and final. It had been a long time since Donald had encountered an opponent that he couldn't either shout down or just bludgeon with his massive fists, but Fergus seemed to be such a one. He was nowhere near as big and muscular as the laird, but the other men standing with him now meant that didn't matter. There were enough of them to do real damage to the laird's productivity but, on the other hand, he was in charge here. And he couldn't – *wouldn't* - afford to be seen as weak. His reply was delivered in a furious rasp. 'If you strike, I'll fire every bloody one of you. I can always find more workers who need the money. Now, turn those machines back on, I'll cut your pay for the week by half and forget this ever happened.'

"Fergus stared straight back. 'Fine, Donald, if that's the way you want to play. Come on, boys – we're striking. Right now.' He strode towards the main doors. Not everyone with him followed, but most of them did. A good twenty in all marched out, the laird's furious shouts having no effect on their resolve.

"The next morning, there was a picket outside the slaughterhouse gates, with Fergus at its centre. A small mob of workers, carrying banners, singing, and firmly stopping anyone coming in to explain their case. Some of those accosted ignored them, but others listened, and either turned and went on their way, or moved to join the gradually-swelling crowd. Donald eyed them irritably, and laid plans to sack them all if their protest continued. He approached Fergus and made his point of view loudly clear before proceeding to his office, in a mix of threats and condescension which did little to endear him to any of them. But he knew that right was on his side. His workers would need money, or get bored, and in a few days, if that, the whole protest would wither and die.

"Donald wasn't often wrong in his business instincts, but this time he was. What he failed to reckon with was Fergus's sheer passion. The lad was young, idealistic, and innocent to the point of naïveté. He believed that such a form of protest would always work. And, with a lot of bosses, it would. But Donald McCrimmon was not like most bosses. All of his life he'd been the big man. Negotiation wasn't his style. He much preferred to beat down his opposition, figuratively and literally. And, like I said, he had one hell of a temper. As the days passed, and the strike didn't end, and as more people gradually joined the pickets, so his irritation grew into anger, blossoming into fury.

"Fergus was the obvious linchpin. His enthusiasm and eloquence were gradually persuading others to join him. So he needed to remove the youngster. And his fury infected his reason – more and more, he saw Fergus as a personal enemy, one that needed to be completely silenced. *Why not just remove the boy, permanently* he concluded. Without him, the backbone of the strikers would be broken, there would be no new firebrand to hold their band together, and he could compel them to his will. Leaving him with only one problem - how to kill Fergus, without being discovered. And, as the cold January of the New Year dawned, he realised exactly how to do it.

"The boy was due to return to Edinburgh a few days before Burns Night. The occasion was much-celebrated in the village, and one of the regular delights was the great haggis made for the revellers that evening. As the foremost local butcher as well as laird, Donald always supplied this, gaining a reputation as one of the finest haggis-makers in the whole country.

"Fergus was surprised to receive a summons to Donald's office that morning, just before the weekend he was due to leave. Neither man was willing to shift in their views, so why did the boss want to speak with him? But that innocence of his won out. *Maybe*, he reasoned, *Donald has finally had a change of heart. Anyone may change for the better.*

"He left the office about an hour later, beaming. He explained to his fellow strikers that Donald had been resentful but also remorseful, agreeing that, while profits were his concern, he had seen the genuine grievances that needed to be addressed, and that he'd arranged to meet with Fergus, at the pub that night to see if an informal accord could be reached to solve the problem. It had certainly surprised him, but he wasn't going to ignore an offer like that. The others urged caution, and he listened, before reassuring them that he wasn't a fool, and that everything would be fine. And he returned to the picket line for the rest of the day.

"That night, Donald and Fergus drank very heavily. The other customers watched them at their table, and felt a certain hope. The two men started by treating each other with guarded respect, then, as more whiskey was drunk, they became more cordial in their manner. They talked a lot, although the others deigned not to eavesdrop, sure that they'd know the outcome if they were just patient. Eventually, the two shook hands, laughing. And then drank some more, and still more, until finally they were singing along with the pub bard, who'd decided to strike up with some tunes. Truly, it appeared that a good drink in friendly surroundings had worked its ancient magic.

"Fergus left the pub very late, with Donald, slurring assurance at his fellows that the strike was almost over, and could very well be resolved on Monday, although he was due to return to Edinburgh on the Sunday, having said his fond farewells to his family and friends the day before. He had tomorrow to deal with any hangover, and urged them to speak with Donald on the Monday, to keep up a friendly pressure. He then staggered off, the laird's heavy arm draped companionably across his shoulders.

"It was the last that any of those men saw of Fergus McNae alive.

"In the earliest hours of Saturday morning, with the sky still black and the moon still high, villagers living near to McCrimmon's factory were rudely awoken. When asked later, they swore that they'd been snatched from their dreams by the sudden roar and grind of machinery – but that it had lasted no more than a couple of minutes in all, before ending as abruptly as it had started. Some of them wondered if it had all been no more than a nightmare of some kind. Those who were sure of what had happened, meanwhile, reasoned that the laird was simply ensuring that the haggis for Burns Night would be as fine as ever. The man guarded his recipe jealously, and was accustomed to making it by himself. *Perhaps,* they thought, *he's making an especially good one as part of his apologies.* And they rolled blearily over and returned to the comforts of slumber. Fergus didn't surface the whole of that day, but the way that he'd been drinking the night before, this surprised nobody. The next day, they knew, he'd be on the dawn coach to Edinburgh before they were even stirring from their sheets.

"Donald arrived at work on Monday morning. Much to the strikers' surprise, he greeted them all cheerily, and assured them that, following his discussions with Fergus, he was sure that an end to their picketing would be reached in a day or two at most. Naturally, they wanted to know what terms had been agreed, but the laird was sly, albeit no less good-humoured. 'Let's just say that Fergus won't have any more problems,' he grinned. 'And that he gave me real food for thought!' These last words caused him to chuckle heartily before he strode to his office. The workers shrugged and carried on. At least it looked like that evening's celebrations would be conducted in a cheerful mood.

"The laird was content. No one knew what he'd done, he'd taken great pains to clean the mincer till no trace of his night's work remained. Oh, there'd be questions about Fergus's whereabouts, but nothing could be proved. Young men often disappeared, like everybody else – running away from home, starting a new life...with no definite evidence, no one could accuse him successfully. And he now had the perfect way to ensure that the youth's mortal remains would never be found. He looked forward to the feast that night, and planned to partake heartily. Meat was meat, after all, and never better than when one had butchered it oneself. And what was good enough for that rugged entrepreneur Sawney Bean, was good enough for him.

"The mansion was crowded that evening with Donald's family, friends, and workers. Everything was going swimmingly: many toasts drunk, many songs sung, many jokes told. Eventually, the laird rose at the head of the great dining-table, thumping his enormous fist on it for silence. As conversations shrank to murmurs and then finally ceased, he strode to the great doors leading to the kitchen, and flung them wide.

"Two brawny servers marched in, bearing an enormous salver between them which seemed a burden even for their strength. On it, the great and noble haggis lay, steaming fresh from its great vat of boiling water. This was clearly a true giant among its kind, and murmurs and gasps of appreciation were heard as it was laid with due ceremony before the laird, the enormous dishes of tatties and neeps all but ignored as they were placed down the table's centre, even the decanters of fine whiskey failing to draw attention from the marvellous centrepiece of the feast. Donald picked up his huge knife, whetting it in anticipation, the broadest of grins splitting his face. As the susurrus of approval faded, he nodded in satisfaction, and poured himself another huge tumbler of drink. This he raised in a toast to the haggis, quaffing a great gulp. The glass was set carefully to his left, the knife was raised ceremonially, and the laird cleared his throat.

"He started on the grand old 'Address To A Haggis' with great ceremony and theatricality, and on the line 'An' cut you up wi' ready slicht', brought down the great blade and cut the enormous haggis open from end to end with a flourish, the rich, steaming innards rushing from the slash, their savoury vapour watering the mouths of all present. Plates were loaded from the dark, moist bounty, and the guests set to with great appetite.

"Donald ate more heartily than any of them, satisfaction evident on his features with every mouthful. The contented grunts and muffled words of praise were music to his ears. The consensus was that this haggis was the finest that any present had ever tasted, a true testament to the laird's care and skill. With more speed than usual, the dishes were cleaned, and a rumble of voices grew around the table demanding more.

"It was while they were digging into their second servings that it happened. As everyone else carried on gorging with evident enjoyment, Donald's wife, children, and his other closest fellows saw him pause. His expression changed from one of greedy pleasure, to a puzzled look of distaste. He swallowed, and then shovelled another forkful into his mouth, chewing this one slowly, and the look on his face shifted into one of near-revulsion. Reaching for his drink, he took another great gulp, forced a smile, and scooped up another great mouthful, and then another, eating with almost grim concentration. His fellows relaxed and returned to their own delicious repasts, until they were interrupted by a loud spluttering.

"Donald lurched to his feet, flushed and coughing. Hunching forward, he spat out his mouthful; then, he froze where he stood, his gaze fixed on his plate with awful intensity. Abruptly, he dashed it against the nearest wall. Haggis and mash splattered. The smashed fragments rattled to the floor. Every shocked eye in the room was fixed on the laird as he gasped and retched.

"With great, panting breaths, he regained his composure, only for his gaze to fall on the splashed food on the wall. His guests watched in bewilderment as his gaze became a stare, a stare filled with shock and loathing. Abruptly, he yelled, 'Damn you, you bastard, leave me be! I'm not frightened of any man, alive or dead!' His wife rose and moved hesitantly to his side, only for him to push her away and square up to the splatter. 'I beat you, boy, like I've beaten so many others. So get to blazes, you wee shite, and don't dare stare at me like that!'

"This display of pugnacious bravado was interrupted, as Donald suddenly bowed forward, and vomited explosively onto the flagstones. He lurched straight again, only for a new convulsion to rack him as he bent once more, and a fresh stream of the stuff rained from his mouth. Still more swiftly followed, even after his stomach had clearly emptied. His wife, children and closest friends rushed, horrified, to his aid. Distraught as he clearly was, he still managed to finally straighten up and stare at the wall once more. 'You haven't beaten me,' he muttered fiercely, 'You *shan't* beat me...' He was repeating these words like a talisman as he was led away to the privacy of his bedroom, leaving behind a roomful of guests muttering in bewilderment. Several of them crossed to the spot where the laird had been standing.

"What they saw caused them to gasp and blink in dismay, rubbing their eyes and looking again, hoping that they'd been mistaken. But the sight remained the same. The splatter of dripping haggis had settled into an image very much like a human face. A face which most of them agreed bore a close resemblance to that of Fergus McNae. A terrible suspicion dawned on a good number of them, a suspicion so vile that it was hard to accept. Many of the guests turned to gaze on what was left of their delicious platefuls, and a good few of them also, suddenly, felt sick to their stomachs. *Had* they been devouring the mortal remains of a young man?

"Those who saw the face murmured in terror to their loved ones afterward. They said that it was definitely Fergus, and that the look on his face was one of furious accusation. For all of the laird's family's attempts to restore a mood of jollity upon their eventual return, without Donald, the rest of the evening passed at best with an air of forced pleasure, and the revels were ended somewhat earlier than usual. No sooner had the last guests departed than servants set to scrubbing the wall until no trace of the image remained.

"Next morning, the laird had apparently recovered from his sickness. He strode downstairs to his breakfast with something of his usual equanimity, a mood which lasted until he saw that a fresh stain had appeared on the wall. Fergus's face, set in its accusing expression. This led to another furious outburst from Donald, as he ordered his servants to clean the wall once more, before stamping off to the factory, only to be met by the spreading nervous rumour among his workers that he had somehow engineered a violent end for Fergus, and had further arranged a particularly vicious way to dispose of the body.

"Much as he tried to quell the rumour, it could not be completely extinguished and he angrily shut himself in his office for the rest of the day. He knew that further enquiries would surely be made, and that it would become clear that Fergus had never left for Edinburgh. He knew that, while this would not provide any definite evidence of what he had done, it would only serve to increase and spread the tale. Determined to end the strike all the more swiftly and harshly, and to come down hard on any workers who kept telling the tale, he made his way home.

"To his fury, he found that the stain was still on the wall, defying his servants' attempts to remove it. He ordered the patch be whitewashed, and sat down to his dinner. Barely had he swallowed his first mouthful when, to his family's dismay, violent cramps once more seized his body until he spewed, continuing long after he had anything to void. It was obvious that the laird was ill, and his wife finally prevailed on him to take to his bed and wait for the doctor. His deputy could keep the business running until he was fully recovered. Reluctantly, he agreed, but refused to retire to bed until he had seen the whitewash applied. 'That'll get rid of you, you little turd,' he was heard to mutter, before he left the room.

"Ill as he was, he was determined to prove that it was no more than the most minor inconvenience, and the next morning he stamped down to breakfast. His family were all looking down at their plates with desperate attention as he entered, not wanting to meet his gaze. When he looked at the wall, he realised why. He had seen the whitewashing, seen the accusing face vanish. Yet here again it was, staring back at his own. Shaking his head in dismissive fury, he marched to the table, snatched up a slice of black pudding, and stuffed it in his mouth. Immediately, his gorge rose. He rushed from the room before his stomach revolted again, but his family heard his retching all too clearly.

'The days that followed saw a grim pattern emerge. Donald would storm downstairs, stare at the face on the wall – he'd given instructions for it to be scrubbed away for a good week afterwards, but the image somehow stubbornly reformed day by day, until the laird eventually gave up on any idea of its obliteration – and address it with quiet fury. Some of his words were overheard, as obsessive and defiant as before... and at last, his family heard him name the image as 'Fergus'. The terrible suspicion appeared to be becoming a certainty.

"And he could never keep down as much as a single mouthful of food. With sickening speed, his great frame wasted away. Soon, he was all but permanently confined to bed, and the finest doctors in the country were summoned. They all examined him. And were all baffled. There was nothing physically wrong with him that explained his inability to eat. They examined him again, and still found nothing. And yet he continued to wither, sustained seemingly only by his unquenchable fury towards the youth that he believed was the cause of his misfortune. More and more, those attending him heard him muttering and exclaiming defiance and hatred of Fergus McNae. Each day, he insisted on being borne downstairs to look at the accusing face on the wall. Each day, his family and attendants became more convinced that the face was that of the boy. Each day, he faced it with fury and invective. Each day, he grew steadily weaker.

"The day that the news came from Edinburgh, that Fergus had never arrived there, was the same one that the doctors made a desperate attempt to keep the laird alive by feeding him through tubes, reasoning that such a method would keep him alive, and possibly even allow for his eventual recovery. But their efforts were in vain, and Donald shook with fresh spasms of vomiting as soon as the first nourishment was fed into his bed-bound body. It was now clear that there was no hope for him in the hands of medicine, and – in secret – his family, increasingly convinced of the true cause of his sickness, urged him to confess all before the face on the wall, and to apologise for what had been done. It took a further three days before the laird, now little more than a breathing skeleton, agreed that he *would* say his piece to the persistent image.

"He had to be carried downstairs, but he somehow found the strength to prop himself against the wall, staring at the face. Drawing a rattling breath, he began. 'They want me to apologise to you, Fergus, for what I did. Well, to hell with that. My way is the right way, and you were a damned idiot to try and change it. I curse you with all of my heart, you stinking gadfly, and by God I'll beat you yet. I will not kneel to kiss the ground before young Malcolm's feet … fuck your forgiveness, I'm too much of a man to be judged by the likes of you!'

"No sooner had he gasped his defiance, than a despairing breath wheezed from his lungs, the last that he'd breathe on this earth. His body thudded to the flags, and the most cursory of examinations proved him to be quite dead.

"The days that followed saw the laird interred with the minimum of ceremony, and increasing dismay in the village as the word of how he had passed, and what he had done, spread. Many who had been at the feast were tortured by their unwitting complicity in Donald's crime, by the potential stain upon their immortal souls. Luckily, the local clergy were merciful, and pragmatic. As none but Donald had become cannibals deliberately, they decreed, those others could not be held guilty. Their ignorance was their defence, and their salvation. But Angus, his oldest son and the new laird, felt that more needed to be done.

"Leading a delegation of family, friends, and workers before the face on the wall, he declared that a monument would be raised to Fergus. Not just a physical one, but a commitment to improving the lot of the slaughterhouse workers, and also that tribute would be paid each year to the memory of the young man who had meant nothing but well for his fellow men, and who had come to such an undeserved end. Not only this: he made a point, slicing open his palm, of making this a solemn blood oath.

"The next morning, the face upon the wall was still there, but those who saw it observed a change. Its stare of accusation had shifted into a smile, a look of contentment. Angus's offer had clearly been accepted – but something about that gaze still gave cause for concern. The new laird was sure that he was still being watched, to ensure that he, and his descendants, were as good as his word.

"And so we have been, Peter, to this very day. The McCrimmon slaughterhouse still stands, and is now one of the safest of its kind, and its workers are respected and well-provided-for. The monument to Auld Fergus is maintained with care in our churchyard. Every Burns Night, he is paid the first tribute of the feast. And to this day ... that look of watchful satisfaction has never changed."

Torcail, his tale told, finished his whisky and gazed levelly at me.

"As I say, you can choose to believe the tale, or not. But, in this village, we believe it. Which is all that matters." He sighed. "Well, the hour's late, and I'm thinking that I need my bed."

I looked at my own empty glass.

"I think you're right. I'll see myself up – and I reckon that I'll take a refill with me. I think I need it."

He rose, a little unsteadily, smiling down at me.

"That's fine with me. Liberty Hall, and all that. But before I go ... in case you were wondering ... pretty much everyone loves the haggis that we make. And there's a very good reason for that. Ever since that night, a century and a half ago ... we've been *very* careful about what goes into them. Good night, Peter."

Halloween

The Last Four in the Bar

Madeleine Meyjes

As always we are the last four in the bar, all leaning on our cues and staring hard at the table before us. The waitress mops the floor, dragging the bucket loudly. She wears a crumpled pair of cat ears over her scowl, the only sign that tonight is Halloween.

Since the kids grew up, I make a point to get out of the house on Halloween. I can't stand the noise or the tacky decorations.

"You're up." Ron nods to me. I can tell his head's not in the game because he keeps glancing at his watch. Ron's a sucker for all this holiday stuff, always has been.

I look at the table and take everything in, already visualising my cue cutting clean through the maze to the '12' hiding behind the '8'. I like the risky moves, the ones that used to make the guys raise their eyebrows - they don't anymore because they've learnt that I always hit my mark. I bend so I'm almost level with the edge of the table and slide the cue.

Somehow, the end nudges the '8' and I have to turn away as I hear it roll slowly towards the corner. Jeff smirks; he's the second best, out of our group, and I can tell he thinks he's going to clean up tonight.

Gregg fishes out the ball. He's always doing things like that for me, always the one who murmurs 'good shot' after my turn. Kind of gets on my nerves sometimes.

As he's walking around the table, I study the green like a map, working out what I can do to redeem myself.

"What the hell?" Jeff says. He's staring hard at a hole that's appeared in the middle of the table. I can't believe it. What a cheap piece of crap.

"I'm not paying for it," I say, looking at everyone around the table evenly. I bet I can get Gregg to pay half.

"What?" Ron asks, then laughs as he notices. "How did you manage that, Stuart?"

"How much do you think to fix it?" Jeff asks.

The others shrug.

"Well, we all chip in, can't be too bad," I mutter. "Of course, I'll pay the most of it."

"Let's just talk about it tomorrow. Stuart, just grab that damn ball and try not to break something else," Jeff says.

I peer into the hole. It's darker and deeper in there than reason allows; there's something red and bulbous in the bottom that looks like a piece of rotting fruit. It moves. I lean over the edge of the table and squint at the shape. I can't believe what I'm seeing. I feel nauseous and have to clutch the side of the table to steady myself.

"What is it now?" Jeff asks.

"It's a prank. It's a prank," I say it twice because the first time my voice comes out weak.

"Very funny, Ron," I say and my voice shakes as I make the accusation. "Festive practical joke. Guess you're never too old, huh?"

"I didn't do anything. What'd you see? Jeez, you look like you're going to pass out."

"Someone else look," I bark. I'm sweating as Jeff leans over the table, I want him to see what I see and yet at the same time I don't.

"Jesus!" He says breathlessly. "How is it... "

At least I know I'm not crazy.

Gregg looks into the hole now and gags. He sticks his hands in his pockets and pirouettes on one foot away from the table. Then he glances around the bar, now deserted, and half-runs, half-strides towards the door. I follow him because suddenly a thousand broken fragments of horror movies are rolling in my head. I won't even let myself put a name to what I've seen, what I think that I have seen.

When I get outside, I watch Gregg retch, leaning against the wall. Even now, in this weird situation, I think he looks pathetic.

Ron rushes out too and I can tell from the look on his face that he's seen what we've seen.

"It's a heart," Gregg says weakly.

I suck the cool air into my lungs and feel calmer. I can feel the cogs in my brain working, I know that what I saw, what I think I saw, isn't possible, so there is another logical explanation. There's always another logical explanation.

"It's moving," he adds.

"I have no idea," Jeff says .

"This is all wrong," Gregg says. "There can't be a heart in a pool table. Still moving. It's not possible."

Ron says nothing. He's still holding the pool cue in his hand and staring at the tarmac. I'm suddenly aware of how forlorn we all look, four little boys scared of some Halloween prank.

"It's a trick, okay? Some weirdo has put a cow's heart in there and attached it to wires or something." I feel more certain of this as I say it. I'm breaking it down in my head, rewinding time and watching that sicko carefully drop the heart into the hole.

"Yeah," Gregg yelps gratefully.

"A cow's heart?" Jeff asks.

"Or something, I don't know, some kind of animal." I search for an image from a butcher shop but all I can see is that thing in the hole.

"Looked kind of human to me." Ron still doesn't look at me as he speaks.

"Human, huh? You can tell the difference? You a doctor now, Ron?" I demand.

"I'm going back in," I say and head towards the door, pissed that they're all acting like a bunch of cowards because of some stupid Halloween joke. Am I the only one with a brain here? This is why I hate this holiday.

I hear the others follow me and even though I'm mad, I'm grateful that they're here. There's something freaky about the bar, now no one's inside, with the blue light from the kitchen filtering through.

I march right over to the table and crouch down. I was so sure I would see some kind of complicated contraption, some home-made Frankenstein-style machine zapping electricity through the board, but there's nothing there but dried chewing gum and scrawled initials. I run my hands from edge to edge one last time, willing myself to find a clue.

"Got to be inside," I say.

"That'll be it," Jeff agrees.

"Makes more sense that way." Gregg joins us.

"There'll be some kind of wire in there," Ron says, nodding.

"Someone help me out here? Why am I doing all the work?" I ask because the thought of touching that thing is making my skin crawl. They're all looking at me big-eyed, waiting for me to fix it, like I always do.

"Who's going in?" Gregg asks.

"Not me." Jeff takes a step back from the table.

Ron is rolling up his shirtsleeves. I'm surprised that it's him.

He inhales like he's about to jump from the high dive then plunges his arm into the hole. He frowns as he feels around.

"Anything?" Stuart asks as Ron removes his arm.

"Weirdest thing." Ron runs his hand over his arm, as if it might have been somehow altered.

"What?"

"Did you touch it?"

"No. I just, it felt like..." Ron struggles to describe the sensation, "It felt like it just went on."

"What did?"

"The space in there."

I approach the table and stick my arm right in, aware of the others watching me. It feels odd, just like Ron described it. It's the feeling of the extra step that you didn't know was there and lights suddenly going out all at once.

"Ron's right, can't feel anything in there. This is some weird shit. Somebody must have thought awful long and hard about this one."

"Think it was that waitress?" Jeff asks.

"Got to be, weird-looking one with all the tattoos and her eyebrow pierced," I say, nodding at Jeff because he's finally decided to start acting useful. I bet it was that waitress. She's one of those goths who always wears black and dyes her hair a different colour each week. I bet she's in one of those weird cults that you read about.

I turn towards the kitchen and the others follow me. I feel infused with adrenaline, like I'm looking down from high up. I feel like someone has shifted my whole being sideways, and now I'm about two inches left of my skin. I can't wait for all this to be over. I'll be sure to remind them of how it was me who took charge and did something about it, instead of running away like some wimp.

There's no one in the kitchen. A fly is buzzing around and the whole room reeks of detergent.

"Hello?" I shout. "You got us! Pretty funny stuff but we've got to get going, so you better come out and clear up this mess."

Only silence greets me.

"I think it's time to call someone, Stuart," Ron says in a voice like I'm an excited child. "We'll tell them there's been a fight, to get them down here, then they'll fix it."

I imagine him calling the cops, of the car pulling up and someone getting out. It would be finished then, we'd clear out and go home. Back to town with all the damned lights and kids swarming the street and the fake real world. But it's getting to me, like a splinter. I need to figure this out, to finish it.

I push past Ron and stride back to the pool table. It looks strangely theatrical underneath the hanging yellow bulb, like a set in the middle of a stage. If I take another look I know something will click, I can feel the edge of the answer. I take a breath and then peer into the hole again. The heart glistens up at me from the cavity. I stare at it, no longer unsettled by the way it beats. I know I'm looking at an illusion. I know I'm at home on my couch, passed out in front of the TV and in this wacky dream.

"What you thinking, Stu?" Jeff asks.

I'm almost out of here, out of this damned bar and free of these useless losers. I'm going to wake up and tell Megan about this dream and she'll say it sounds like a good sci-fi movie and we'll laugh about it.

I notice Ron in the corner, huddled over his cell phone and Gregg murmuring to him. This is all taking too long, I'm itching to wake up and get out of here. I open and close my eyes, willing myself to consciousness.

"What you doing, Stu?" Jeff asks. He's standing too close, like I'm going to protect him.

I knock my fist hard against the side of the table, hoping the pain will jerk me out of this. I'm still all too here, in this weird limbo, and its making my chest tight.

Apart from the heart, everything feels normal. I want dancing alligators and the bar to become a forest. I want it to be to be over.

Maybe it's the heart. I just have to get rid of the heart, like some challenge I've set myself to wake up. It's one of those meaningful dreams Megan's friend Ellie always speaks about, the ones I always thought were crap. Maybe she was right though, like this is me overcoming my fear by getting rid of this thing.

I weigh the pool cue in my hand, holding each end gently. If I hit it from straight overhead, that should finish it, quick and clean. I practise raising the cue over my head and bringing its point down.

I take a step back, lifting the cue with both hands and plunge it into the hole.

Blood spurts everywhere, more than I thought possible. It sprays over the green of the pool table and splatters my shirt and even my chin. I pull out the cue and stare at the heart impaled on its end. It looks like a ridiculous prop.

Jeff turns from the table and vomits. Gregg and Ron run to the table, yelling at me but I can't understand what they're saying. I can't believe that I'm still here, that it didn't work, that there is a heart in the middle of the pool table.

It doesn't make sense.

Things quickly happen. Like Ron taking the cue from my hand. Like Gregg and Jeff grabbing the bleach and cloths from the kitchen and scrubbing the table, the floor, themselves. Like hands grabbing my arms and pulling me up. But I do not wake up.

Then I walk outside and hold my keys in front of my car door for a while, not wearing a jacket but not feeling the cold. Then I drive home and sit in front of the house and don't notice the noise or the kids or the lights.

***

I trudge upstairs, pausing on each stair, telling myself to go forward.

"How was it?" Megan asks, as she flosses her teeth.

"Fine. It was fine," I tell her from far away.

I undress slowly, carefully and find comfort in my neatly-folded rows of shirts. I unbutton this shirt and toss it in the laundry basket. I hear the sound of a ball rolling. It seems to come from somewhere on me.

I search the pockets of my jeans for my keys, although I am sure I left them downstairs on the hook. Then I step out of my socks and pants and leave them in a heap on the floor.

The sound increases as I move. It becomes louder as I strip off my vest and stand in front of the bathroom mirror. I have the oddest feeling that the noise is coming from within me. I shift from foot to foot, there it is again: the sound of a ball, rolling. I've heard that sound before, the clean noise of plastic against wood. Almost, but not quite because this time it is not wood it meets, but bone.

Vallum Hadriani

Justin Newland

Tullus wanted to scratch his back. But he couldn't reach beneath his heavy tunic, as his arm movements were restricted by the breast plate and armour. By Jupiter, his back still itched. All the same, the scratches reminded him of Morgance and better times.

His sword made a grating sound as he rammed it into its sheath. Gloved hands against icy rungs, he climbed the ladder and emerged onto the watchtower. The low rolling hills were covered in a pall of white by another snowfall. Dawn was oozing out of the horizon. With the new recruit from Gaul was Marius, his nemesis.

"So, the Praetorian is awake," Marius snarled.

Since his disgrace, these jibes had been his daily fare for a year. They were like an open wound and sometimes he wearied of trying to stem their flow. Mostly he took his barbs during the day and, one by one, removed them at night from his mind. Only scars remained.

"I'm confused," the Gaul said. The boy wore a down of fluff on his chin. The Roman army took them young these days.

"What about?" Tullus asked.

"If you're a Praetorian, why are you here guarding the vallum?" The Gaul asked. The tinge of awe in his voice betrayed a respect for the fierce protectors of the Emperor.

Before Tullus could reply, Marius swooped.

"Don't let him fool you, Allum," Ah, so that was the Gaul's name. "Tullus doesn't guard anything. Instead, like some ghostly numina, he floats around the snows of Caledonia.

And he's the worst kind of ghost - he's a deserter," Marius prodded the air with a lean finger.

"No, I'm not," Tullus insisted for the thousandth time. Yes, he'd left his post but it was for good reason. The trouble was no one believed him - least of all the Emperor, whose life he'd accidentally endangered. Now these frigid hills and dales were the bars of his prison.

"*Praetorian Tullus* wasn't forcibly conscripted like you and me," Marius continued as if he wasn't there. "No, he was once a member of Hadrian's vaunted guard."

"Yes I was and, no matter how much you goad me, you'll never take that away from me."

"Once our mighty Tullus protected Consuls, slept with their wives, and beat their servants. Today it's his duty to keep a watchful eye on an unfinished wall and a ditch full of dirt ... when he's not sleeping with his whore," Marius said, making a rude fist.

"She's no whore," Tullus said, his voice as cold and hard as frost. The barbs were digging deep.

Marius jutted his chin at him with utter disdain. "I'm a Brigantes and even I wouldn't poke Morgance."

"You're mad," Tullus said, vapours of anger rising before his eyes.

"*I'm* mad?" Marius snapped back. "Then how come no one's ever seen her?"

Tullus pulled out his dagger and lurched at Marius. In a flash, Allum stood between them, one arm pressed against Tullus's chest, the other against Marius's.

"Stop this," Allum snarled.

"By the gods," Tullus said, panting and sheathing his dagger. "One day, I'll vindicate myself. I'll show you I was right all along."

"Of course you will. Now start your watch, coward," Marius spat the word out as he descended the ladder. Allum threw Tullus a look of confused disdain and followed the Brigantes. Typical Marius, coming like a bat out of the twilight and then vanishing.

Tullus was alone. He escaped to the place where he always went for solace - to Morgance. In his mind, he conjured her sleek body and imagined her pressed close to him. His reverie was interrupted by the distant sounds of men marching, hundreds of boots crunching the ice-bound road. Along the wall at the nearest milestation, the men from the Second Legion were already heading towards him to start the day's construction work. Until they arrived, he, Tullus Maximus Gordanus, was the vanguard, the sole guardian of the temporary end of the long curtain of wall and ditch that snaked out from one coast and reached towards the other. This was the nearest he got to the days when he basked in the warm brilliance of the task of guarding the most important man in the world.

To keep from freezing on the spot, he trudged the turret perimeter. His breath was steamy and his hands already numb from the cold. Dawn was casting splashes of crimson across the frozen landscape. Even he, a Sardinian far from home, bore a begrudging appreciation for its stark, homogeneous beauty.

He peered down to the ground at the base of the turret and noticed track marks in the snow. They came from the north - the Picts' land - and stopped in front of the turret. They weren't Allum's; he'd have come from the east, by way of the milestation. Why hadn't Marius spotted them during his watch? They didn't look like foot prints or paws. He descended the outer ladder to take a closer look.

He was right. The tracks were freshly made and were neither human nor from any animal he recognised. Three undulating lines, one above the other, they were like waves in the sea. Wait. By the Vestal Virgins, they were the same marks. As last year. Not again.

Memories of his disgrace flooded back to him from when the Emperor Hadrian had visited these parts to commission the wall. That morning, Tullus had followed the same wavy lines into the woods, convinced they warned of impending danger. He tracked them as far as a rock near a frozen pool, where he'd encountered Morgance - an alluring undine with flame-red hair. Entranced by her beauty, he'd strayed from both his path and his duty.

Out of that slither of opportunity came a hoard of Picts. In a wave of blue death, they wreaked havoc on the milestation, disembowelling men, and raping women. After a bloody battle, the Picts were repulsed. A pyramid of skulls was gruesome testament to the Romans' retribution, which made Hadrian's clemency to Tullus even more surprising. Mitigated by Tullus's exemplary service to that point, the Emperor had condemned him to spend the rest of his days chained to the scene of his great mistake: the wall.

Since then, Morgance had stayed out of sight of prying eyes and sent him dreams that soothed his anguish. She'd made him feel like a man and slowly, he'd grown to trust her again.

They were *her* tracks. She said she'd help him restore his pride and position. She was sending him a sign. *This* was it: the Picts were coming. They'd wait until dusk and swarm through the rising evening mists. If he discovered the enemy's dispositions, he'd redeem himself.

He strode off to the north towards the forest, his hands, and feet like frozen lumps of stone. So much white. The silence, pristine. The forest, thick. The path, winding and narrow. Bare trees. In a clearing, far-off, he glimpsed a band of Picts, prickly as thistles, plotting, goading each other on.

He had to return - before the Picts attacked. He crept away, silent as a snow flake, and stumbled into the forest's beating heart. A frozen pool ... a rock ... a woman. Beguiling. Beckoning. It was Morgance. There she was. She would rescue him. He never felt so much joy, so much relief. He lay down and felt her wings embrace him. He lay back in ecstasy.

***

Tullus awoke to loud voices.

"Can you still see his tracks?"

It was Marius. At last.

"I'm over here," Tullus shouted.

"This forest is going to devour us - it's alive with spirits," Allum was saying. "Come on. Let's get back to camp. Tonight is the last night of Saturnalia. The Centurions will serve everyone at dinner and I don't want to miss that."

"Forget it. You'll be the dish being served if we don't find the deserter," Marius replied.

No! That wasn't right. He hadn't deserted. Not again.

"Over there, the Picts are mounting an attack," Tullus yelled. "Can't you hear them? Can't you hear me?"

Marius's torch was sending flickering lights around the trunks and branches. Macabre shadows danced on the frozen pool. As dusk settled, the owl of Minerva spread its wings.

"Allum. I found him. He's here," Marius called out.

"Help me, I can't move," Tullus pleaded with them, but they definitely couldn't hear him.

Allum said, "How did he end up slumped against this tree?"

Marius kicked him hard in the thigh. His body crumpled and fell limp on the ground. Strange, he felt no pain.

"Stop that," Allum protested. "Don't the Brigantes show respect for the dead?"

"We do," Marius scoffed. "When they deserve it. Listen, as part of his punishment, Hadrian had him whipped to the edge of death. Tullus convinced himself the wounds on his back came from wild love-making with Morgance. He was obsessed. She was a spirit who only existed in his dreams - she was numina."

"Well, now they're numina together," Allum said.

January 16th

Dark Time

Clare Dornan

George stood in his hallway, listening to the tick, tick, tick of the antique carriage clock. He opened its small, domed glass door, took hold of the clock's metal hands and yanked them so hard they bent out of shape. The clock ground to a halt.

He gazed at the silent machine, sighed and slowly began his morning routine. He buttoned up his cardigan, slipped on his thick wool coat and wrapped himself in his scarf, fur-lined hat and black leather gloves.

As he stepped out of the house, he hunched his shoulders against the icy wind that always whistled up his street. He walked steadily with his eyes down, half-closed, barely registering the route to work. He never met anyone to talk to and the village looked so drab in the mornings. Everything was muted and bare now that it was stripped of its festive colour and the dull-grey January sky lay heavy and close overhead.

At the shop, George had his morning chores timed to the second. He knew that, at a steady pace, it took him one minute and thirty-five seconds to unlock the shop door, switch off the alarm, raise the security shutters and boil the kettle in the storeroom downstairs. That left him with three minutes and twenty-two seconds to drink his first cup of tea and be back upstairs and standing in the large window of Barker's Antiques and Curios, before Mrs Charrington arrived at 10.03am.

Mrs Charrington always opened the door at exactly the same moment - and once inside she would pause, unclip her large red handbag and retrieve a handkerchief to wipe the rain from her glasses. George waited patiently for her to put them back on - he knew from experience that she grew unsettled if he spoke before she could see him clearly.

"Good morning madam," he said quietly.

She looked up and smiled. George stepped forward and casually rested his hand on a small oak cabinet positioned between them.

Her eyes lowered and then widened in surprise.

"Oh, is this what I think it is?"

"If by that, you are wondering if this is a Robert Thompson original? Then yes, madam it is. A very beautiful piece, but, sadly" — he paused for effect — "it is missing the other parts of the set."

'But I have a wardrobe in that style at home," she said, her face alight, "and a tallboy! I never even knew that - "

"Really? Well, well, madam, that is quite something. And are you looking for the third piece in the set?"

"Goodness me. Well, I didn't know there was such a thing, but it is such a dear. I've had the other pieces since my mother passed away some years ago – though she knew nothing about antiques. She only had them as my aunt ..."

George allowed Mrs Charrington to begin her explanation. He knew the exact point in her morning dialogue when she had relaxed sufficiently to buy the cabinet – but he could spare himself the details of her entire family.

He waited for that right moment and then interrupted.

"I'm looking for £1750 for the piece. And you are welcome to take it straight away. If that would suit you, of course."

On some days, he sold her this piece for £3000. Occasionally he had even given it to her for free, just to see her reaction. But now he chose the price that delivered a fast and painless transaction, as the novelty of conversing with Mrs Charrington had worn off a long, long time ago.

Once he'd waved her goodbye, he stood staring out the shop window onto the village square. At 11.29am, the clouds would darken and sleet would send huddled figures scuttling past his shop. No one, though, would enter to browse his collection of Antiques and Curios until two German exchange students came in briefly at 3.12pm.

It was at this point in the morning, when he would often try to recall how many times he'd lived through this exact day. Really, how many times must it be now? It was enough that he couldn't remember. Enough that he didn't care to know any more.

All he was sure of was that every day when he woke it was Monday, January 16th, 2012. Every morning, the same grey clouds hung overhead. Every morning his house was exactly the same; his fridge contained the same food in the same place and his coat hung on the peg by the door, even if he hadn't left it there the night before. Every morning the antique carriage clock in the hallway would be tick-tick-ticking, no matter how thoroughly he'd silenced it. And every day the oak cabinet would be once again unsold, in the window of Barker's Antiques and Curios, ready for Mrs Charrington to make her discovery.

He slowly descended into the storeroom – a large, dimly-lit space, crammed full of boxes and dust-covered furniture. His father had accumulated the vast collection over the many years he had owned the shop. His father had been a natural hoarder, but he had also had an eye for things that could sell.

It had been with the hope of finding valuable treasures amongst the vast hotchpotch of items that George had begun sorting through the storeroom one January weekend. Late on the Sunday evening, far later than he had intended to stay, he'd found, stashed in a far corner, his father's collection of clocks. Six large cardboard boxes overflowed with wristwatches, fob watches, silver watches on chains, alarm clocks, carriage clocks, large wooden wall clocks and even small free-standing grandfather clocks. George, like his father, had always enjoyed trying to fix these old machines, bringing them back to life, and he'd quickly picked out the ones that caught his eye until he'd been surrounded by clocks.

He'd sorted the last of the boxes, when he became distracted by a glint of metal amongst the dust on the floor by the far wall. He reached through a cloud of old spider webs and picked up a small metal box. The surface was tarnished and badly scratched on one side, but when he turned it over, his eyebrows shot up and he gasped. In his hands lay a clock with a delicate, translucent, pale white face, tiny black hand-painted numbers and hands made from plaits of golden wire. The base of the box was a small piece of clear glass. He grabbed a microscope from his toolbox and peered closely into the heart of the tiny machine. It looked like the inside of an M.C. Escher painting – an elaborate, intricate maze of tiny, interlinking cogs.

He turned the box over, expecting to find a key to wind it up, but there was nothing. He used his pliers to prise open the glass panel and attempted to physically turn the cogs with the smallest screwdriver he had to hand. The mechanism refused to budge. He dowsed it in oil and continued to prod and poke, gouging the teeth of the tiny golden wheels, until slowly, like the waking of a drowsy beast, a few of the cogs started to turn. He rammed the screwdriver in hard, forcing the cogs to turn faster until he heard the first reluctant Tick.

The second hand moved. Lazily at first, but gradually it picked up pace. And as it did, the ticking grew steadily stronger. George smiled, transfixed, as the entire maze of golden cogs started to glitter and spin. He had hoped to find a prize in the vast jumble in the storeroom, but he'd never dreamt of discovering anything quite this beautiful. He was amazed that his father had left such a rare piece damaged in the far corner of the room. Surely a clock of this value, would have also caught his eye?

He pondered this very question, until he became aware that the ticking sound was surprisingly loud and the entire room reverberated with a steady, mechanical pulse. He held up the small clock in surprise, but then his eye caught sight of an unexpected movement by his feet. He stood and slowly turned, his mouth falling open in confusion. The collection of clocks he had assembled surrounded him in a perfect circle. And they were all kicking out the same constant ticking beat.

His hands gripped the small clock, tight with fear. Her voice sliced through the room,

"You just couldn't help yourself could you."

"You couldn't leave well alone. You had to tinker and meddle. Just like your father"

He spun, but could see no one.

"Who's there? What are doing down here?"

Her voice came again, this time louder, closer.

"Did you ever wonder what happened to your father, George? Hey, little Georgie? What happened to dear old papa?"

George squinted into the semi-gloom, desperate to locate her.

"Get out of here," he shrieked, "This is private, you're not allowed in here."

He kicked a path through the circle of clocks at his feet and stumbled towards the stairs out of the storeroom. She sat on the steps, waiting for him.

"Going somewhere, Georgie?" she said calmly.

He froze at the sight of the tiny figure. She was the size of small child, cloaked in a white dustsheet with straight golden hair covering her face. Her hair glistened and heavy drops of oil slid down her locks onto the storeroom floor.

She raised a thin, delicate hand – not a hand of flesh, but fingers of twisted, plaited, golden wire. She slowly moved the hair from her face, instead of eyes there were two white clocks with black hands spinning furiously.

She drifted closer. George stood frozen rigid, with the small clock held tight in this hands.

"Your daddy couldn't leave me alone either," She said. "Didn't you find it strange how he just disappeared? One day he was here and then... puff... oh, dear! Daddy's time ran out."

As she spoke, George could see her mouth was filled with a mass of whirring, spinning, glittering golden cogs.

"I don't like being so rudely awakened. Time is not always at your beck and call." she spat.

George hurled the clock, at the tiny figure. It flew straight through her and crashed into the wall.

***

He had no memory after he'd thrown the clock until he woke the next morning, safe in his bed at home and the grey dawn of Monday, 16th January, 2012 had begun. He'd innocently presumed, on that first Monday, that the hallucinations from the night before were nothing more than a mixture of exhaustion and hunger.

Now, so many Mondays later, he climbed over the boxes and found the small clock, where it had smashed into the wall. He collected his tools and slumped over his workbench. He prised open the clock. But what to try this time? Over the countless Mondays he had cajoled, oiled, prodded, carefully restored and totally destroyed it, but never again had the clock sprung into life.

Tears of frustration streamed down his face and he couldn't help but wonder. Somewhere, trapped in another point in time, his father also sat in this storeroom, day after day, doing the very same thing.

Love and Christmas

Thomas David Parker

Beth watched Will as he placed the roasted goose in the centre of the many dishes of the Christmas feast.

The logs crackling in the fireplace made the room cosy, a perfect accompaniment to the gentle choral music coming through the discreet speakers in the corners of the hall.

"My God, Will, this looks amazing!"

She grinned as he spun and caught sight of her standing by the door. He smiled in response. Beth teased a lock of her long, black hair so it stroked her cleavage, to draw his eyes into her glittering emerald dress. "There's no way we can eat all of this!" she gushed.

"Well, at least give it a go," Will said grinning. He pulled out the chair at the head of the table for her. "What we can't finish, we can have for leftovers tomorrow."

"You mean, you're not going to cook for me on Christmas day?" Beth stuck out her bottom lip playfully and blinked her extended lashes. Will looked sheepishly at his feet for a moment and smiled awkwardly.

"Of course I will, darling. Anything you want to eat tomorrow, you can have."

"Please can I have pancakes... with bacon? And... ice cream?" Beth asked. Will's awkward smile fell slightly but recovered quickly.

"Shall we just focus on one meal at a time, my love? Glass of wine?"

Will picked up the decanter and Beth beamed, as he poured. Will took his seat opposite. They were distant from each other, for the table stretched the length of the hall, but it was an experience that Beth had always wanted and he seemed happy to oblige. Despite never enjoying cooking or spending time at his country retreat (he preferred sampling the fine dining available in the city), he knew the significance of the evening and wanted to fulfil all of Beth's wishes. They both raised their glasses and said 'Grace' with a laugh. Beth gulped a long, swirling mouthful.

As her tongue stirred the wine around her mouth, Beth noticed a slight tingling and burning sensation. She swallowed instinctively, but this just spread the burning down her throat. Beth began to feel light-headed and struggled to catch her breath. She glanced across to Will, who seemed to be watching her sympathetically. Searching his eyes for an answer, she tried to speak, but only croaked. Tears filled her eyes as the room faded and she heard Will mutter,

"There, there, my darling. It'll be over soon..."

***

Beth opened her eyes and found the pain had gone. In fact, there wasn't any sensation at all. She spotted Will, kneeling at the fireplace, stoking the fire, which wafted a strange aroma across the hall.

"What's going on?" She asked, shocked at how strange and hollow her voice sounded. Will turned at the noise.

"Ah good, you're up!" He said with a smile. He stood and wiped his hands on a rag. They were soaked with blood.

"What's happened... What's happened to me?"

Will paused, clenched his hands and took a breath.

"Ah, well actually... I'm afraid to tell you that you're dead."

"What?" Beth jumped up in alarm and noticed the partial remains of her body slumped beneath her. There was a bloody trail leading to the fireplace and the source of the strange aroma was revealed. She stumbled in shock but, without any tangible form, she fell through her chair and then sank into the floor. She screamed, unable to comprehend what was happening to her.

"I'm sorry, but it's for the best," Will shouted, attempting to be heard over her screams. "Please try and understand. This is a good thing!"

"A good thing?" Beth yelled. "What the fuck are you talking about?" She was beginning to come to terms with her predicament and was far from happy.

"Don't you see? We get to be together forever now, and you don't need to worry about aging anymore. You were always concerned about getting wrinkles."

"You murdered me so I wouldn't get wrinkles?" Beth gave Will a death stare. He swallowed with an audible gulp. She had managed to crawl her way onto the surface of the floor, realising she could move herself with an intense focus.

"No, it's not like that. Well, it's partly like that, but it's mostly just to make sure we're always together." He looked away from Beth's glare. "D-don't you understand, you get to enjoy all of the best bits of our relationship, without any of the bad bits."

"You're not making any fucking sense, Will. I'm dead. How am I supposed to enjoy the best bits of our relationship?"

"Because you have me!" Will said. "You were so busy before, with work and friends, but none of that matters now that you're dead. We can just focus on spending time together!" He gave her a child-like smile.

"You're insane," she said. "Completely insane." She shook her head, her thoughts in chaos, and she struggled to focus. "What about the sex, Will? We won't be able to have sex any more, have you considered that?"

There was silence. Beth's anger diminished slightly, as she was embarrassed at the ridiculousness of her question. However, Will didn't seem to notice and he smiled, as he answered her.

"I have. Of course, I have, my darling, but I realised it doesn't matter. Our relationship was more than just sex. Anyway, we didn't do it that often because you never seemed to enjoy having sex with me." Will gulped again at Beth's continued silence. "You kept coming up with excuses; you were always too bloated, too tired, too near your period or on your period. There never seemed to be a right time when you were in the mood."

"Plus, you were having sex with James, from work".

Beth span to confront the spectral form of a middle-aged woman who'd interrupted.

"W-Who are you?" Beth asked "And... and how do you know about James?!"

"I'm Will's mother," the spirit said, "and I've been watching you for a long time. I needed to make sure you were right for my son."

Beth's fragile grasp on the situation almost collapsed. But the rage she felt, the injustice of a frankly-ludicrous situation, helped her maintain her grip.

"So, because I was sleeping with someone else, you felt it was perfectly acceptable for your son to murder me?!" Beth's anger built to a level she had never felt before; anger at her death, anger that they knew her secrets, anger at her lack of power, anger over the fact her lover had become her murderer and she hadn't even realised she was dating a psychopath.

"If you didn't enjoy sex with my son, why didn't you leave him?"

"Because I was scared!" Beth screamed. "James doesn't love me, but at least he makes me feel good. Will always guilted me into doing stuff for him.

"He was so manipulative that I thought he'd kill himself if I left. I didn't know he was such an evil bastard. If I'd realised he never loved me, I would have left ages ago!"

"It's not like that," Will said, a tone of exasperation creeping into his voice. "Why won't you understand? I did this because I love you."

"Even though I was fucking another man?"

"Yes, but I forgive you. It was obvious by your texts you were just using him to fulfil that physical attraction you didn't have with me. But now you don't have a body, so you don't have that physical desire anymore. It can just be the two of us!"

Beth searched for possible escape routes, but this wasn't her house and Will and his mother seemed so calm, she felt powerless in their presence.

"How is this possible, why is this happening to me?" She had moved backwards as her instinct to run propelled her spirit, but Will and his mother calmly matched her pace and maintained their proximity.

"Fifteen years ago, when my father died, I discovered I could see his ghost," Will said. "I'd never seen any other ghosts before, but I guess the emotional connection has to be strong for it to work. It was amazing to discover this gift and know that my father was still around and still part of my life.

"We would talk a lot, but it was difficult to tell people because no one else could see him. The only person I tried to convince was my mother, because father missed her so much, but she thought I'd gone insane."

"I didn't think you were insane! I was just concerned that your grief had caused some temporary hallucinations," Will's mother said with an awkward smile that emphasised the family resemblance. Beth stopped, her fear replaced by a morbid fascination at this new side to Will and the situation she found herself in.

"Anyway," Will continued, "my father missed mother so much, he suggested I take her life so she could join him as a ghost and see that I wasn't crazy. I was a little unsure at first, but she was always so angry at me every time she caught me talking to father, it made me feel anxious all the time. I love my parents and I hated mother thinking I was crazy, and I eventually saw that father's plan made sense. I would be reuniting my parents and proving my sanity. Mother would be better, father would be happy, and I would be too. So, it was a fairly easy choice and I smothered her with a pillow."

"Hmmm," His mother muttered. "You know, I wish I'd been poisoned. Smothering sounds alright, but it's not as quick as they make it look in films."

"I know mother. That's why I used poison this time," Will said with a sigh. "As I was saying, it felt great to see them reunited. However, what I didn't know was that I was only connected to one ghost at a time. Shortly after my mother died, my father disappeared. I guess he passed on. It was devastating for us both, but at least they got to see each other one last time and mother got to see I wasn't crazy."

"And I've been with him ever since, as his guardian angel," his mother said.

"But weren't you angry that your son had murdered you?" Beth asked. Will's mother smiled as she put a hand on Beth's shoulder. "I must admit that, like you, I was quite cross when I first discovered he'd killed me, but then I had to accept he did it for the best of intentions; I wasn't the nicest person to be around in my final days. And you have to admit that, with your lifestyle, you can be a bit high-maintenance too." Beth clenched her jaw and swiped the spirit's hand off her shoulder. Quite cross did not cover the rage she felt, and she felt it growing, as she learned more about the true extent of their insanity.

"Don't pretend you did this for your son. You did this so you could pass on to the next stage of the afterlife!" The words had an impact on the spirit, but not in the way Beth had intended. There was no guilt or shame in her response. It was more a hardened resolve.

"Well, I couldn't be the only woman in his life forever, could I? I've been stuck with him for fifteen years like this and I deserve my peace. It's not as if I've been lazy in all that time: I've been helping him to find the perfect person to replace me, before I can pass on. Someone who can keep him company, someone that he can love and who will love him in return.

"I was so pleased when we found you. Now, you can't begrudge me wanting to pass on and be reunited with my husband, can you?"

"But what about me, you expect me to stay with Will for the rest of his life while I'm like this?"

"Oh, you'll figure it out, can't you see that you still get to spend time with the one you love?"

"Will?"

"Yes! Don't you love him?"

"No!"

There was a silence after that confession. They both turned to Will and saw the betrayal and embarrassment burn across his fallen features.

"Well, I'm sure you'll figure something out." And with a shrug, Will's mother began to fade away, until there was nothing there but empty space.

Will was silent and motionless as Beth tried to think of something to say.

"I'm sorry," were the only words that escaped her lips.

"For what?" replied Will, fresh tears welling up in his eyes.

"What do you mean?"

"Be more specific." Will's tone had shifted. There was a hard edge now, that Beth hadn't heard before, and it scared her.

"For saying I didn't love you."

"Did you ever love me?" Will's eyes locked with hers for a moment, until Beth was forced to look away.

"Of course, Will. But you murdered me. People who love each other don't murder each other." Beth felt she was losing power in the conversation, but she couldn't understand why.

"But I love you," Will said. "And I murdered you so I can spend the rest of my life knowing you're with me."

"But why me? Why do you want to spend the rest of your life with me?"

"Because you're smart, and I find you interesting. You're beautiful, and you'll never age a day. And you're spoilt, so it's about time you put someone else's considerations before your own."

It was Beth's turn to be silent and motionless. Will had revealed exactly what he thought of her and suddenly everything was brought into sharp focus. He hated her. He said he loved her, but he had written her off as a spoilt princess and then used that as justification for her murder. Fury began to build at her core, but it was a cool white fury that she was able to control.

She didn't think Will understood love. He saw it as possession. She was his trinket, a pretty thing that said interesting things, but not a real person with a complex set of emotions. Her desires didn't matter and that's why he didn't care about her cheating on him with James.

Now she realised it was because it wouldn't fit with the narrative he was making for her, the convenient, spoilt, little rich girl that he could justify as his ghost bride for the rest of his life. Someone who didn't deserve to live, but would be a good companion. Someone that, if he spoiled her enough, would see him as a saviour and love him unconditionally, because Will only saw women as gold-diggers.

Beth understood her affair with James supported that narrative, but the truth of the matter was that she had only slept with him because Will was terrible at sex. He was the selfish one, always finishing first and never ensuring that she climaxed. He never even thought to ask!

Will believed he had all the power once she'd died, but when she'd said she didn't love him, it had cut him deep. "Why do you think your father only appeared to you and not to your mother?" Beth asked.

"What?" Will said, confused.

"Why did your mother never see your father after he died? You said you thought it was because the link was strong between you, but wouldn't it be stronger between man and wife?"

"I guess so. I never really thought about it."

"You never thought about it? You had the ghost of your mother with you for fifteen years and you never spoke to her about it?"

"No, but I don't see what you're getting at."

"Your mother didn't love your father, not like you did, and that's why she never saw his ghost. The connection wasn't there."

"Shut your mouth, whore!" Will screamed and lunged, but passed straight through her and crashed to the floor. The fall winded him and he let out a choked sob. Beth watched him as he regained his breath and composure, but there was fear in his eyes now. "I'm so sorry," he said. "I didn't mean that. I just got upset and..."

"I know," Beth said. "I was trying to provoke a reaction, I'm sorry. I knew you couldn't touch me, Will. You're tied to the physical world. Only a spirit can touch another spirit."

"I can't believe I tried to hurt you," Will said, as he rose to his feet. "There were difficulties in my parents' marriage, but I always tried to ignore them. You always want to believe your parents love each other, don't you?"

"I'm sorry my words hurt you," Beth continued. "But I'm still coming to terms with my death and having no body," Beth's words were calm and measured and she made sure she had a look of sorrow. "I do love you, you know. I just spoke out of anger and hurt because I was scared. It's weird not having a body. If only you knew what it felt like."

"I will, eventually."

"But don't you think this is unfair? That you get to have a physical body and I don't. If you really loved me then you'd want us to be equal."

"I do, I do. And we will once I die."

"So why not die now?"

"What?" Will looked at Beth, but she kept her face was expressionless.

"Isn't there some poisoned wine left?" she asked, offering an encouraging smile as she approached him. "Yes."

"Then drink it and join me. Show that you love me. Show me we're equals."

"You want me to kill myself?" Will took a few steps back until he bumped into the dinner table. He looked down and saw the decanter of wine next to him.

"If our connection is as strong as you say, if you're joined to me and my spirit, then don't you want to touch me? C'mon Will, prove that you love me," Beth moved closer until she was only a few inches from Will's face. "Don't you want me to touch you? Don't you want to kiss and make up?"

Without a moment of hesitation, Will grabbed the decanter and took a large gulp of wine. He looked at Beth and she smiled back. Will's body slumped to the floor and his spirit rose to meet her.

"Together at last," Will said as he took Beth's hand. "Together forever."

"Thank you," Beth said and kissed him on the lips. "And Merry Christmas."

Will felt the kiss linger on his lips. He looked at Beth and saw tears fall from her eyes. It was not a kiss of passion as Will had hoped, it was a kiss of farewell. A kiss of sadness, tinged with pain. He watched as she faded away, leaving him with nothing but an empty hall and the remnants of their final meal. Will was left all alone. There was no-one left; no-one could see him, no-one could save him and no-one could hear him, as he began to scream.

Retribution

Suzanne McConaghy

There was something satisfying about the idea of visiting my mother's grave on the tenth anniversary of her death. I needed to mark the event. I wanted to tell her how far I had come since I had got free of her.

The road skirted the cemetery. My calves burned from the unaccustomed exercise as I followed the wall that snaked up the mountainside, through the rapidly-thickening mist. Everything in this town went steeply upwards or downwards, with altitude sickness a possibility for the unwary visitor.

Every twenty feet or so, the wall was punctuated by an embrasure with a seat. I smelt tobacco. On the third one, a girl, smoking. Leather jacket, tiniest of short skirts, red lacy bustier, four-inch heels — you get the picture. I felt a stab of excitement just looking at her. Was that red hair, bound up in the flimsy scarf? She was relaxed, as if it were a summer's day. Clearly, she didn't feel the cold — or else, she had grown used to it, plying her disgusting trade, trapping unwary men. These girls deserved everything they got.

She stood up and smiled when I appeared out of the mist — a broad, welcoming smile, as if she had been waiting for me. Well, this was quite something! For a moment, I wasn't sure what to do. That's unusual for me. I had no plan and planning is something I take seriously. But she had no hesitation. She grabbed my hand, fingers icy.

"Come into the cemetery. I know a good place, out of the cold."

"What's your name?"

"Ana. And yours?"

"Why do you need to know?"

"No reason. You asked first."

"It's Eduardo."

"Come on, then."

A part of me just wanted her, although I don't go with prostitutes. Mind you, she didn't look like the whores I'd seen hanging around — too healthy for a start. And that smile was enticing. I felt desire growing. This was completely unexpected — but why not profit from it? She could see I was still unsure, however.

"Well, if you're not interested..."

I made up my mind. I could have her and my wife would never know. It was important to me that my wife have complete confidence in me — I couldn't risk anything else. She was my shield. It was ironic; usually, when people have sex at conferences, it's with fellow delegates. You don't have to go looking for a prostitute. But it's dangerous to entangle with other attendees, not least because there's a chance it'll get back to someone who knows you. So this seemed too good an opportunity to pass up. Then she said, "Let's see your money," and that brought me back to reality. It was a transaction. What was I getting worked up about? We agreed a price and she said that if we continued around the wall, there was a way in.

The iron gate, with its scrolls and curlicues, stood ajar. As we crossed the threshold, a bank of thick fog rolled down from the mountain and onto the path, obliterating everything around us. Even the crunch of gravel beneath our feet was suddenly muted.

Nevertheless, I felt I was being watched. I stopped and put my finger to my lips. We waited. I could hear drops of water falling from the branches and the scuffle of some small rodent beneath the bushes — but nothing that seemed remotely human. What was strange, and was beginning to affect me at some level, was not being able to see anything. Even while holding onto the girl, I couldn't see her other arm, or the handbag she clutched. I had never experienced fog so dense.

"Where are we going?"

"Be patient, we're nearly there."

She led me to an elaborate folly with an enclosed space that was situated above what would be a family mausoleum. It was a large structure, in the same overblown, baroque style as many of the tombs, but much more imposing because of its size. It was covered with vines and screened by them on three sides. We climbed up a short flight of steps. She was right; it was much warmer inside, even though the fog was everywhere. There was a bright, red-patterned blanket spread on the floor.

"You've been here before."

"That's right. No-one else seems to have found it. I think of it as my own place."

She pulled me over to the seat.

"Sit."

She sat next to me and looked deep into my eyes before pressing herself up against me, inviting me to take her. Her eyes were fathomless, her exposed flesh cold and soft as snow. A shard of pure desire coursed through me. *Dios,* she was a luscious piece.

"I like the idea of doing this over all those dead bodies," I said, beginning to press and push against her swelling mounds, while her musky scent assailed my nostrils. "What a clever girl you are! It definitely spices it up for me." I squeezed her breast hard, intending to hurt and then put my hands around her throat, enough to make her feel uncomfortable. You have to make sure they know who's in control. She shoved against me and stood up, breathing heavily, but there was a smile on her face.

"Just wait here a moment, and I'll find something else to spice it up!" She ran lightly down the steps and vanished behind the matted vines.

I waited on the stone seat, thinking, sufficiently aroused to enjoy the anticipation. I'd had a lucky break. I wouldn't be here if it weren't for the climate change conference. I've made alternative energy my life, had my work featured in *New Scientist* and *Scientific American,* and recently *Semana* had written a flattering article about my newest project. It meant my work was important. I felt I was on my way — and about time, too! I knew I was good. Just occasionally, I allowed myself to dream a little, about how my government might ultimately recognise my efforts.

I strained to see through the fog. She hadn't returned. Where was she? Five minutes later, I was seriously irritated. I don't take kindly to people playing tricks on me. I'd punish her for this when she got back. Perhaps... my thoughts wandered along pleasurable paths, mainly concerned with making her see the error of her ways. I knew how to make a girl pay for her wrong-doing. I'd had plenty of experience. But, after twenty minutes, I had lost patience and felt the anger flood my being. She wasn't coming back.

I dropped down onto the path. She had aroused a whole slew of feelings and desires that I could do without, especially when I had a paper to give the next day. I hadn't wanted a prostitute, had I? I'd passed up on the ones by the hotel without a second glance, as they offered their damaged bodies in the freezing mountain night. How dare she treat me like that? It was always the same. It didn't matter how hard you tried, people couldn't appreciate the fantastic opportunities you gave them.

My heart beat too fast, choking me. Rage was building. I picked up a marker stone from the side of the path and hurled it. It thudded against something hard, metallic even, and I felt a tiny surge of satisfaction. I imagined how it would have been if I'd heard her cry out in pain. I'd have caught her then. I could see myself slapping her, punching her. She deserved that. Maybe, afterwards...no matter.

I calmed down. Nothing achieved by losing your cool. I was already in the cemetery and I *would* visit my mother's grave — it was the only opportunity I would have because I was never going to be in Santa Maria again. If it was the last thing I did, she had to know how successfully I'd escaped her. There was silence all around. The last of the family groups, honouring their dead, had long disappeared. I couldn't see an inch in front of me. But it didn't matter.

All those Sundays after mass during my childhood, visiting *Abuela*, my grandmother. The old witch. I could have found the grave in my sleep.

I trudged onwards, anxious not to fall or twist an ankle. Out of nowhere, there came a great clicking, fluttering noise and a huge swarm of creatures encircled me. Bats! I hate them, disgusting things. Some were sitting on my head, others darting at my face. I put up my hands to protect my eyes, tripped over one of the markers and went down my full length. I felt my head strike against some large object and blacked out.

When I came to, I was lying face down. My mind was blank but my head was pounding so hard, I wondered if I was suffering from a hangover, although I couldn't recall drinking. As my senses returned, I felt the cold in my limbs and knew I was out of doors. Then I remembered where I was. Could I risk a look around? Cautiously, I opened my eyes. Excruciating pain. I quickly closed them.

There had been no sign of the bats. Groaning, scarcely able to lift my head off the path, I turned onto my side to heave myself up onto my knees. I didn't know anything about the habits of bats but do any creatures go flying around in thick fog? Surely not. I didn't understand what the significance was – and I don't believe in coincidence. It would take a lot to convince me that the bats had sprung up from nowhere, at the very moment that I happened to be passing. Something had caused that to happen.

I could've sworn there was someone else in that damned cemetery, right there with me, and not just Ana. I'd thought I was being followed even before I'd got there. I remember the shock of the cold, dark night after the warmth of the hotel foyer. I'd walked briskly, sure I was alone but I'd had that disquieting feeling that you get when you're being observed.

People tend to react when they realise the eyes of others are upon them — although, from the careless behaviour seen everywhere nowadays, it would seem that many people have lost all awareness of possible danger. They don't understand how important it is for self-preservation. But of course, in such fog, that couldn't be the case. I must have heard something.

When I came to a large tree, I stood to its side, waiting, concealed from anyone walking by. I heard no-one. Finally, I had to admit that I must have been mistaken.

But was that the case? Was there someone out there after all?

There was a bench to the side of the path. Sick and shaking, I slumped onto it. If there was a murderous person about, I needed to be alert. Tears squeezed themselves out of my eyes. Someone was after me. Someone was trying to kill me. How could that be? I knuckled my eyes, forced myself upright. Where would they come from? I swung around. Maybe they were just behind me? I punched out into the woollen blankness, again and again.

But there was no-one. I couldn't believe the treacherous bitch had dared to do this. I hoped she'd been attacked by bats as well! Why had she taunted me like that? Anger burned through me, a searing flame. *Just you wait, Ana! I'll find you, wherever you are. You won't get away with this. I will kill you.*

I sat there for a few minutes, freezing. I heard no-one, saw nothing.

I felt all over my head, looking for injuries, and my hands came away covered in blood, black and sticky in the curious silver-grey light of the fog. More blood dripped down the side of my face. I needed medical attention. Finally, the dizziness began to recede and I struggled to my feet.

The far corner of the cemetery, where I knew I'd find my mother's grave, was much higher than where we had come in. The path wound between the tombs and gravestones, climbing up the mountainside. Ten minutes later, I came upon her burial place.

My mother had a proper tomb, not just a common gravestone. Death was a family affair — five generations of De Silvas lay in its mouldering depths. And, as far as I was concerned, they could stay there. Jones was my dead father's name. Ese Galés, they'd called him, with infinite disdain. 'That Welshman,' as if mother hadn't had a hand in choosing him in the first place, as if his Welshness explained everything that was wrong in her life. He hadn't been allowed a shelf in the tomb. They'd buried him where he'd died, in Cartagena, and refused to tell me where his grave was or even what had caused his death.

While I'd worshipped my father, they'd tried to blacken his name. I'd been six years old when he died, leaving me to the tender mercies of my mother. From that moment on, I never heard a good word spoken about him, nor did I receive a single kind gesture from anyone. It was only later that I wondered about the family possibly having a hand in his death. I picked up a long-stemmed red rose from a bunch a family of mourners had carefully placed on their grandpa's grave. A stolen rose: a fitting tribute for my mamá. Then I headed for the looming shape in the far corner.

I was almost blind, the fog chill and unpleasant, but I'd recognised the pretentious stone pavilion, with its iron gratings and the white marble statue of the angel on the top. I walked around it, my mind full of conflicting thoughts: anger and triumph at what I had achieved in spite of her. As I laid the rose on the step, I noticed the door was open.

Now, there was no reason why that should be, unless vandals had broken in. I believed myself to be the last surviving member of my family — and who else would visit the grave of the vindictive, sour-faced old harridan who called herself my mother?

Then I saw the door move. I couldn't swear to it, not with the poor visibility. I tried to see through the streamers and tendrils of fog. Suddenly, there she was, right in front of me — my dead mother! I took a swift step back, raising my hands to defend myself, the way I had done as a child.

"You always were a coward!" There was no mistaking the voice, strong and vibrant. Wasn't she dead? This was crazy; it must be some long-lost relative. She looked like my mother, though. She'd had a sister, right? I'd forgotten about that.

"She persecuted me." I had spoken in spite of myself. "She beat me. She took all her frustration out on me because she couldn't hang onto Papá."

"You're a vicious and cold-hearted coward — which you proved when you killed me."

"Mother, I didn't..."

"Don't waste your breath. Don't even bother. I *know* ."

I held back for a moment, fighting the rage I'd always felt when she started in on me. How did she manage to affect me like this?

"You always tried to control me. Why've you always hated me?"

"Because you're weak and you're a killer. Only the weak have to kill, to make a point. But I won in the end, oh yes! Look at what you are now."

"I don't understand you. I'm a respected member of the community. I do good, make the world a better place. I haven't..."

Mother smiled. She *smiled*, the evil bitch, all her ignorance and snobbery and ridiculous prejudices on show. She couldn't begin to understand the things that I did. I realised she despised the work I was involved in, as if I was merely the local postman or a greengrocer. It wasn't good enough for the De Silva family.

Her voice cut into my thoughts.

"Couldn't you stop, after you murdered me? You got a taste for the blood, didn't you, like your father? Killing me, over and over again, through all those others? I tried to beat it out of you, God knows, once we knew about him. Maybe I was misguided."

How *dare* she talk about my father like that? I was so incensed I leapt towards her, maybe intending to cut her throat. I don't know. Immediately, the fog wrapped itself more closely around her and she became difficult to see, but the unmistakeable sound of her cruel laughter echoed. I trembled. She'd always had that effect on me, reducing me to less than nothing. I felt exposed. I patted my pocket, checking the knife was still there.

There was no way I was going to put up with this. I made to go, but another form materialised from the fog.

"She's right, you know, or I wouldn't be here."

Shit! The kid — the street kid in Bogotá. It was her dark red hair that made me choose her, hair exactly the same shade as mother's, so unusual in Colombia. In seconds, blood flowed and it was the colour of her hair in the darkness. There was a rightness about it: she was my sacrifice to the gods, a thank-you to them, for helping me get rid of mother. A worthless street kid.

"You don't matter. What use were you to anyone else? No-one missed you. Terminating your miserable little life allowed me to continue my work for three productive, peaceful years."

Saying nothing in reply, the child climbed onto the tomb and settled down to watch me.

"You've forgotten about me, I expect." I swung around. "Half an hour of so-called passion with you and all I got was dead. It's Ester, that's right — a common prostitute. You didn't even know that, did you? How well you repaid my generosity! I was so pleased to see you, after all the dirty weirdos I'd had to deal with, that I invited you back to my room. There you were, a nice, clean young man. How could anything go wrong? How naive and foolish I was!"

A surge of excitement ran through me as I remembered how wonderfully and deliciously things had gone wrong for her. The film in my head unrolled: I pierced pale flesh and angled the knife upwards. I felt myself growing and swelling as power entered me once again.

She wafted off to the left, draping herself against a self-important stone lion, her long, red hair fanned out over her body. Was this a show, with me in the starring role? If so, it was getting out of hand.

"I've never understood what *I* did to you." The old woman, with the traditional bowler hat and pleated skirt of the mountain women, looked at me with the eyes of a wounded animal. Why did I choose her? The need had become insistent, that's why. And I hadn't found any redheads. She was there, peddling ribbons and hair products on a street corner in Bogotá.

I followed her when she left her pitch, heading towards the outskirts of the town. I was going to do it, whatever the colour of her hair. I was starting to despair of finding an opportunity, when an abandoned warehouse loomed on the right, its door hanging open. I shoved her in and, minutes later, it was over and I lay, satiated, on the grimy floor. The hollowed-out shell I had become slowly filled with life and power, making me whole again. I remember I pulled off her hat. Long red strands came lose from her hairpins. Had the colour come from one of her bottles? I didn't know and, as the rush came, I didn't care.

It's the aftermath of each event that's clearly etched on my consciousness, the tremendous boost to the system, which might last a matter of months, or even a few years. Wrinkly old bag. She wasn't worth thinking about now. None of them were. Who did they think they were? Did they seek expressions of regret, an apology? I lunged at her but she drifted away and sat on a gravestone, at a distance. I pocketed the knife. I must be losing it if I thought I could kill her a second time.

"Nice of you to drop by on All Soul's Day and give us the chance for conversation." The skinny girl — the drug addict, I remembered her now — appeared from behind me. I'd come across her outside a nightclub. The red hair again, and then...

I suddenly took in what she had said and my heart thudded in my chest, constricting my breathing.

All Soul's Day? What was she talking about? I checked my iPhone, feverishly pressing buttons. ¡Madre de Dios! there it was, November the second, the Day of the Dead. How could I have missed it? Of all the days to choose to come to my mother's grave! I remembered something about communion with the dead. I had to get away.

"Well, this farce has gone on long enough." I turned on my heel. "I'm going."

"Not so fast!" Mother again. "There's a debt to be paid."

"What debt? Oh, you think I should care? No chance. You did your job too well, mother. I'm the same as you."

I ran towards the exit, the spirits and ghouls screaming and screeching behind me, and I cannoned straight into a solid figure by the gate.

"Stop right there, you miserable piece of shit!"

"What...? Who...? You're making a mistake."

"No mistake. I've been following you. The police have known about you for a long time. Couldn't prove anything – until now, that is."

They thought they knew me. How arrogant. I felt the wave of rage again.

"What rubbish is this?"

"We saw the pattern. When we discovered you would be attending the conference, we were sure there'd be another murder. We knew you'd try again, sooner or later. Ana used to be a prostitute, you know. She was a friend of Ester's. That made it personal for her, you see, so she was willing to help. She saw you that night but we had to make sure."

He held up his phone. "I've got it all here, Jones; your confession, all recorded. Very obliging of you to confess on your mother's grave. Mind you, we didn't expect that — we thought you'd chase after Ana and try to kill her. Maybe the spirits took a hand to help us."

"That's not evidence! It's entrapment. You've got nothing on me."

"Except Ana didn't leave the cemetery. She's a witness. She heard every word you said. Eduardo Jones, I am arresting you..."

"I don't know what you are talking about," I said, snatching up a spade leaning against the gate post. I'd beat him down and use the knife to finish him off. The open tomb would be an excellent place to hide him and no-one would know. Already my body was throbbing, anticipating the release I would feel as the knife went in. It had been fifteen months. I struck the first blow, hitting him hard, flat on the side of his head. He stumbled backwards, groaning.

"I'll kill you. You'll never get me. I'll fillet you into little pieces and—"

"No, you won't." They grabbed me from behind and wrenched the spade away. Uniformed policemen. I was surrounded. They shoved me face down into the wet gravel and I felt cold metal as handcuffs clicked into place.

January 6th

Epiphany

Margaret Carruthers

First night. Two days to our anniversary. Laura cooks for us. I sleep. I dream.

I'm walking along a street when two figures, a man and a woman, approach. They try to speak, but I can't hear any words. The woman starts to move towards me, putting her hands on my head. I scream. I wake screaming.

Second night. The eve of our silver wedding. Laura cooks again. Neil is irritated with her for not leaving us alone.

I'm walking along the beach. It's a clear, sunny day. The tide is turning. I can see the waves slowly advancing towards me. I stand watching the surf when I see the familiar couple approaching me. They face me. The woman, looking desperate, reaches towards me. I scream. I wake to find myself in Neil's arms.

Third night. My stomach screams in pain. Neil is unconscious. Laura smiles from the doorway.

I'm standing at the top of a cliff. The couple stand between me and the edge. The woman has a single tear running down her face. I turn around. I will face Laura.

I wake.

Winternights

Maria Herring

"If the lights go out..."

"They will not, All-Father," said Rathgithr. "You always bring the lights back."

"Look at me," said Odin. "I am defeated. The lights will go out. Ice, fire and chaos will rule." Rathgithr shook her head, searched for words to deny this truth. Odin found his words first. "*Look at me!* They have done this. You were right, my foster-daughter, but I heeded you too late. Now you must stop them. Stop them, so the lights come back."

***

The sun set on Winternights, a bloated blister on the western horizon, its last light bleeding away into eternity. Yet the dying day heralded, as always, the start of the Wild Hunt.

In the east the sky grew blacker, not from the passing of light; from the frenzy of black horses, black bucks, black hounds, darker than death, deeper than hate, their eyes hideous with knowledge. A wild tantivy came from Asgard to Midgard, from the divine realm to the mortal realm, filling the vaulted heavens with howling winds and battle cries. Down from Valhalla, Hall of the Slain, rode Odin All-Father with his furious host. Nine valkyries astride their steeds, swan-feathered cloaks clapping as thunder, shields ripping the air. Nine spectral warriors rode also, great in life, greater in death, hand-picked by Odin for this nocturnal hunt. Finally came the black tide of stolen souls, crashing back in love and loathing to lands once walked, screaming their despair, for only the restless dead can inspire fear in mortals during Winternights, the darkest half of the year.

And while the unrelenting darkness smothered the lands and the baying winds and galloping storms broke the eerie silence of midwinter, the cold was absent. The gales had not teeth of ice but hammers of heat. The air was filled not with squalls of snow but floods of ash. And water trickled where frost should shine.

***

"First fire of Winternights, my little Vikings, time for stories."

"Not this year, Jarl," said Hanna, throwing another log into the flames, wincing at the heat. Only nine people left this year; the summer plague had been brutal. Even so, her husband insisted on carrying out these ancient rituals. "No stories. They scare the children."

"Hey! Only Agata gets scared. I don't get scared, I'm a man now."

"You were scared last year, Bjorn, I remember. You wouldn't let Daddy put out the fire."

"Shut up, Agata."

"That's enough, you two." Hanna spoke to her children but looked at her husband. "If you're going to tell your stories, try to make them a little less gruesome."

She set herself down between her mum and her sister. Five months had passed since Hanna's brother-in-law had died and her sister's anger still bubbled close to the surface. She couldn't accept that their mum's skills at healing were dependant on the ingredients she had to work with—and they were fewer day by day. She gazed down at the meagre catch for tonight's feast and suppressed a sigh. Some feast. These rabbits were as skinny as her children.

"Then less gruesome they'll be, my love. And so! The first night of Winternights—"

"My granddad said they called them Nuclear Winternights in his day."

"Yes, Filip, you tell us every year. Can I continue—"

"Only it was much colder in them days, my granddad said. And darker."

"You tell us that too. Now shut up, Filip."

“I don’t like the dark, Mummy.”

“That’s because you’re a baby.”

“I won’t tell you again, Bjorn,” she said, fixing him with her warning eye before turning it on her daughter. “You can come here and help us skin the rabbits. Here, do this one.”

“Urgh! We can’t eat this. It’s only got one head.”

“Stop talking, all of you! It’s time for Winternights story-telling! Thank you. And so! The first night of Winternights is when the old god Odin comes back with his army of monsters and ghouls to terrify all the survivors of the Great Blast...”

***

A moon-turn of searching and the raging host had yet to find a settlement of mortals. Odin All-Father had called a halt to the ride and spectral warriors and valkyries alike scoured the land for new souls to claim while their midnight beasts searched for prey. Neither souls nor prey were found and the nine chosen slain were restive.

“Where is the blood?” roared one, known in life and death as Erik, rattling the tokens on his belt. “Mortals will hide this bleakest half of the year, yet still we find them. There are always souls to take and corpses to make. Where is the blood?”

And Odin All-Father, flanked by his ravens, replied, “I know not. While answers elude me, observation does not. Each Winternights yields fewer mortals, this I have seen.”

“Fewer mortals,” said Freyja, Odin’s wife and Mistress of the Slain, “and warmer climes. We are summoned to Midgard every Winternights, but where is winter?”

“And where is the God-bridge?”

This last came from a shield maiden. Rathgithr was her name, which means counsel of peace. Up in the skies she searched, looking for the Reddened Ways of silent-coloured lightning that linked Asgard to Midgard; the Bivrost Bridge. A memory of it remained, no more than that, a path on its way to forgetfulness.

“If it leaves here,” she said, “how do we?”

The black beasts howled in hunger. The furious host sought answers in each other's eyes. Yet unlike the beasts, they found no sound to make.

***

Rathgithr regarded the wounded wing of the blood eagle sprouting from Odin's back, decorated as it was with feathers of Memory and Desire, and sought to reign in her fear. She failed. She was witnessing the death of the All-Father.

"I cannot do it alone," she said at last. "Let me free you from this. The shield maidens have left us, but Freyja will help. Together we can stop this madness. Let me cut you down."

"I can see them too," said Odin, his voice distant as laughter's memory. "The eight other worlds now in this one. You were right, Rathgithr. All nine worlds are here. I see them now. Had I only heard you before when there was time. Now there is no time. Is there any left to ask for your forgiveness?"

"Let me cut you down," said Rathgithr. Once again Odin heard her not.

Rathgithr wept.

***

"And who can remember what Winternights is?"

"The time when you get all my grandad's stories wrong."

"Shut up, Filip. I was talking to the kids."

"Don't get them started again, Jarl," said Hanna, raising her warning eye to him this time. Bickering, she thought. I seem to spend my dark days stopping people from bickering. Bickering about food, bickering about the plague, and now bickering over stories. I wonder if there was ever a time when life wasn't just one unending bicker?

"It's when the world went cold and dark, Daddy! And then it's Yule presents, and then the sun comes back, and then it's spring and Winternights is finished. I'm right, aren't I, Daddy?"

"I knew that too, but I let her answer, otherwise she'd cry because she's a baby. I also know that we don't have winter and spring any more because it's always warm now. And I know Winternights actually ends because Odin died on some tree and came back to life and brought the spring with him."

"Well done, Bjorn!"

"Thanks, Dad. In your face, Agata."

"I knew that too! You just said that because you're ugly!"

"Yeah, well, you're stupid *and* ugly!"

Hanna rubbed her temples. Every year the same. She couldn't wait for Winternights to end.

***

A moon-turn more. While the warriors scoured the skies with Odin, the battle maidens stalked the lifeless plains below. Still no mortal was rooted out.

"I weep to see this world thus," said Freyja. "Have we come back when all the mortals are gone? Is this Ragnarok?"

"We are the blood-covered prophetesses of Odin," said Rota, one of the nine foster-daughters of the All-Father, and she was blood-covered indeed. Beneath armour of bone her pale robes were crimson and her arms were decorated with bracelets of teeth seized from battlefields. "Were this truly the end of all things then we would have seen it already. While Asgard is unchanging, this one blighted with ephemeral mortals is inconstant, for they seek to make their mark on it before they are forgotten."

"I see marks," said Freyja, "though I see no mortal making them. I tell you, Rota: I look at this world yet I see Muspelheim's fires."

"Pah!" Rota hammered her shield. "Let us call this Ragnarok then. Where is Surt with his flaming sword and his Devourer kin? Twice the moon has fattened and shrunk yet the fiery death of the gods hides from his destiny? I say no to that. I say you see end times because you see change."

"I see them," said Rathgithr.

"What do you see?" said Rota, turning on her. "Devourers? End times? You lie. You see nothing."

Her words were brave to Rathgithr's ears, though she heard fear, saw that fear flicker in Rota's eyes.

"I see all nine worlds," she said. She feared the sight would fray her mind but she would not blink, for she also feared the sight would be lost. From this mortal realm, the nine boughs of Yggdrasil, the World Tree, branched out to eternity before her eyes, bringing all the realms into sharp focus: Asgard and Vanaheim where the divine ruled; Alfheim and Svartalfheim of the Elves and Dwarfs; fiery Muspelheim and frozen Niflheim; Jotunheim of the savage Devourers, and the dead realm of the goddess Hel.

Distant as the flickering stars they were, yet she saw each blade of grass, tongue of flame and feather of ice. She felt the tremors as the great hammers of the dwarfs fell to their artifice. She heard the laughter of the elves as they plotted their mischiefs. She smelt the burning air, the frozen air, the dying air, the pure air of all nine worlds together. She perceived that she could touch them all, should she reach out her hand to do so; she knew that so doing would topple her into the void.

Her senses were wakened for the first time and she trembled with rapture and fear.

"It cannot be true," Freyja whispered. She stepped so close to Rathgithr that her alarmed breathing rustled the hair framing the shield maiden's face. "Please, tell me it is not true."

"You need only look," said Rathgithr. "If I can see it, so must a goddess with knowledge such as yours."

"I am afraid to," she said, her eyes squeezed shut. "For if the ways of the worlds are open to all, it swans me that doom is upon us all."

These words chilled Rathgithr more than the coldest Winternights had. She, too, closed her eyes, however once the worlds were seen they could not be unseen. And she knew that now the way was open, it would not be shut.

"Do you believe," she said, her voice faint in her own ears, "that this is the reason no mortals remain here? Have they perished as all things must at the ending of the worlds?"

"Do you ever listen to your own words?" said Rota, stalking towards them. "They are soft, Rathgithr, as you are. Ever you have chosen the weakest from the battlefields, the farm boys who only fought because their king forced them to. You chose fumbling peasants over great leaders and now they sit amongst their betters at the tables of Valhalla—you brought shame down on all your sisters. And now this?"

"Bravery is not counted by the number of dead left on a battlefield," said Rathgithr. "It is continuing on a path, no matter how fearful."

Rota scowled, disgusted. "So this is *your* bravery, is it? Filling yourself with fear and calling it changed destiny? I called us blood-covered prophetesses, but you—pah! Your pristine swan feathers and silver armour do not have even the faintest spot on them, white maiden. You do *nothing* yet you would change everything. It is not just your words; your whole being is soft, *Peace*."

"I will not be goaded into another argument about my choices, Rota. I am not the only one who senses doom here; our mistress does too."

Both maidens looked to her. Before Freyja could answer, the warm black air filled with the trumpeting cries of victory. As one, the choosers of the slain and their mistress looked to the sky and saw Odin astride Sleipnir, leading his spectral warriors down to the plain.

"They have succeeded where we did not," said Rota, grim with satisfaction. "It swans *me* that the ritual of the Wild Hunt can finally be undertaken at last."

Rathgithr turned to her mistress. She could not recall ever feeling fear before. She saw fear in others, when their lifeblood soaked into battlegrounds of their own making and she did not choose them to live amongst the deathless warriors in the Hall of the Slain. Feeling it was a new sensation. It was her flesh torn open and her nerves given to the elements. It was her soul forced to answer the pleas of the desperate dying. It was immortality in the void.

"If there are yet mortals then we must leave them be," she whispered to her mistress. "Without them, there is no mortal realm."

"And if one realm falls," said Freyja, "the others will follow."

"Pah! This is folly not foresight," said Rota. "You think Odin would not know if this were the Fate of the Gods? He would not lead us into the Wild Hunt if it meant the end of us. The All-Father would know."

"I did not know," said Freyja. "Not until Rathgithr opened my eyes."

"I see nothing," said Rota, and Rathgithr heard bitterness in her voice. "You seek to ruin the old ways for nothing."

"I seek to save, not ruin," said Freyja, then raised her voice. "Gather around your mistress, shield maidens. We must decide how best to halt the Wild Hunt so that these are not the last Winternights we ride."

Rathgithr, her heart a trapped moth in her breast, gazed around at her foster-sisters while debate rattled amongst them as hailstones. One after the other, however, their eyes were opened and the boughs leading to the other eight worlds appeared before them. Then all eyes save one pair reflected the disquiet that Rathgithr felt, and the expression only deepened when devising a plan to halt the hunt came to naught.

"We slay the chosen," Rathgithr said, as abruptly as the idea came to her.

"Treachery!" cried Rota. "I will have no part in it!"

"No, it is not *treachery*," said Rathgithr, the moth charmed by a flame of hope. "They are the chosen slain. When they fall in battle they wake again in Valhalla."

"That is well thought!" said Freyja. "Let us speak to my husband first. If we cannot convince him with words, then I will use other means to blind him. Then, my shield maidens, you will know it is time to send the chosen slain back to the halls."

***

"...which is when zombies come back to eat the all the naughty children by ripping out their—"

"That's enough, Jarl. We're trying to eat. And you've made Agata cry. What did I say about making your stories less gruesome?"

"They're supposed to be. It's tradition. Don't you think it's important for the kids to learn about their traditions?"

"Not when it makes them cry, no."

"My grandad said that Odin came with great big horny women, not zombies. Where'd you get the zombies from?"

"Shut up, Filip."

Hanna looked up suddenly. It was always windy, but it seemed to her the clouds boiled more than they ought to. And it was probably just because of her husband's retelling of their ancient Nordic myths, but she could've sworn those clouds had faces.

***

"We have found them!" Odin cried, his voice a thunderclap in the storm of triumph. "We have found brief mortals cowering in their bowers. Ride with me, corpse maidens, and we will show them what it is to fear the darkness!"

"There are yet mortals?" said Rathgithr, the flame burgeoning.

"Yes! Three men, three women, three children. We ride to battle!"

"We must not, All-Father," she said. "They are too few. I see the nine worlds and Freyja senses our doom. If we steal the souls of these remaining mortals, then the lights will not come back for this world after the hunt. Should that come to pass, all worlds will remain dark."

Odin reigned in his eight-legged mount before her and she quailed in her lord's presence. None who gainsaid the All-Father remained in Asgard to speak of their mistake.

"I always bring back the lights," he said, his voice rumbling low, his ravens landing on his shoulders to glare at her. "You deny us the hunt?"

"I deny you nothing," Rathgithr replied. "But I ask you to consider: what will we become with no mortals here to fear us?"

"We are gods and the riding dead," he cried, his chosen cheering his words, flaunting axes and spears. "They are only mortals. They are here for our pleasure. They are here for our hunt!"

"And if they are the last," said Rathgithr, "if they are taken from this realm so that it falls, what will become of the remaining realms? Do you think the hunt will endure when the boughs of Yggdrasil are fallen into the void? All-Father, I beseech you, open your eyes and see what your wife and foster-daughters see."

So Odin looked. Rathgithr was certain she saw the first flickering of understanding dawn in the All-Father's eyes, but before the flame flourished into a beacon it was doused by the battle cry of Rota.

On feet fleet as thought, she tore towards the chosen nearest her, sword already swinging, voice impaling the night as her blade impaled him. Flesh ripped and blood sprayed; before a drop fell upon the scorched land the spectral warrior vanished back to Valhalla, where he would wake ready for battle once more.

But not this battle.

"We would steal your hunt," Rota screamed at the boiling warriors, "and save the mortals. Now we choose them instead of you."

And she turned to Rathgithr and smiled. She continued to smile even as a brother of the slain hacked at her with his axe. She even smiled as her corpse fell to the ground and the ragged mouths of her wounds smiled too. With the last strands of her life she had woven a web of war and crossed it with a crimson weft.

It was a war one-sided, for the battle maidens merely chose the slain, they did not create them. The spectral warriors, however, grew rabid at the sight of immortal blood, howled to set their blades gnawing like wolves on the valkyries' armour.

Rathgithr watched as her sisters raised impotent shields against honed blades, stood their ground while undead death raced towards them. Throughout eternity they had witnessed battles uncounted yet never had the sisters fought one. Bravely they stood, too easily they fell, as harvest wheat to the sickle, as the tears down Rathgithr's cheek. And even as she saw her own doom rush towards her, she heard the All-Father cry out:

"Spectral hunters! My foster-sons! Cease this slaughter! These shield-maidens are not your prey! There is wisdom in Rathgithr's words, for I, too, can see the boughs of—"

"*Women's words?*" roared Rathgithr's doom, halting before her in a spray of ash, turning to the All-Father his nightmare face of fury. "You would use women's words to undo a hunt that has raged since the beginning of all time? That will continue to rage until the ending of all time? You are no Father if you would stop your sons from spilling the blood they exist to spill."

An armoured fist eclipsed the nine worlds and Rathgithr saw no more.

***

Silence came first. The silence that comes after a great storm or battle, silence that describes its ending, and the devastation left behind. Rathgithr opened her eyes, surprised that she still could; they were gritty and tight from tears dried slowly in warm air.

Sound came next. The baying of beasts far off, distant as a fading dream; closer, a sigh, mistake-mournful, a zephyr's threnody to lands stained with maiden's blood.

"Rathgithr."

She knew the voice, knew it well, for it came from her foster-father and it had spoken to her forever. She dragged herself to her feet and beheld the end of all things.

Upon a parody of a tree made from the corpses of her sisters, their arms entwined and twisted into boughs, their legs splayed as sprawling roots watered with their blood, Odin was fastened and fettered by the entrails of his daughters. But that was not the end of his hurts. His back was cut and his ribs outspread into the gruesome wings of the blood eagle, made more offensive by the addition of the begored wings of his ravens, Thought and Desire, unfolded for flight, halted in death.

"Rathgithr," he said again through bloody lips. "If the lights go out..."

"They will not, All-Father," said Rathgithr. "You always bring the lights back."

"Look at me," said Odin. "I am defeated. The lights will go out. Ice, fire and chaos will rule." Rathgithr shook her head, searched for words to deny this truth. Odin found his words first. "*Look at me!* They have done this. You were right, my foster-daughter, but I heeded you too late. Now you must stop them. Stop them, so the lights come back."

"I cannot do it alone," she said at last. "Let me free you from this. The shield maidens have left us, but Freyja will help. Together, we can stop this madness. Let me cut you down."

"I can see them too," said Odin, his voice distant as laughter's memory. "The eight other worlds now in this one. You were right, Rathgithr. All nine worlds are here. I see them now. Had I only heard you before when there was time. Now there is no time. Is there any left to ask for your forgiveness?"

"Let me cut you down," said Rathgithr, but once again Odin heard her not.

Rathgithr wept, for Odin wept. "Freyja has left us too. They left us nothing. You *must* stop them, Rathgithr."

And so, she saw the relics of a goddess. Deified she was in life for her love and beauty, her wisdom and knowledge. In death she was sundered, torn apart by hands of hatred, ravaged by savage beings ruled by blood lust in death as they were in life. No face had she now for Rathgithr to know her, nor form to recall the glory of her living splendour. The Mistress of the Slain, her foster-mother, was slain indeed.

Anger swelled within Rathgithr then, pushing out her sadness, until it thrashed within her, hotter than the gales of this dying world.

"I will stop them, All-Father," she vowed. "You need only tell me where they are."

***

"What's a raven, Daddy?"

"A type of two-headed chicken."

“Oh. Well that’s not very special. We’ve got two-headed chickens and we’re not gods.”

“We haven’t got chickens, genius, they’re rabbits.”

“Well if you’re so clever, Bjorn, why aren’t chickens rabbits then?”

“That’s enough, Agata. Both of you. Can you hear that, Jarl? What is that?”

“Nothing. Just the wind, my love.”

“That’s the not the wind. It sounds like... Jarl, I think it’s voices.”

“Them’s not voices. My grandad said there’s not been people here since—”

“I think we should go back inside now. Come on, children, up you get. Quickly now.”

“But Mummy—”

“Now, Agata! Into the house right now!”

***

Odin had found the mortals, three men, three women, three children, on the last of several hunts with his warriors and so Rathgithr knew her path. But even without the All-Father’s whispered words, she would have known, for the shroud of stolen souls that ever accompanied the Wild Hunt boiled in torment, shrieking their loss, plaguing the last settlement of mortals with their despair.

They swirled around her, pulling her hair, tugging her armour, leading her to the place she must go. She knew she was near, for dread consumed her anger, dread that arrived when she perceived no sounds of battle, telling her the chosen foster-sons had wreaked their havoc and urged the hunt on in their insatiable quest for blood.

Odin’s was not the only blood eagle she found on this last day. At the entrance of a crumbling settlement of wood and stone she found one man, one woman, one child speared to leafless trees, wings of blood and bone protruding from their tortured corpses; three eagles of the hunt plucked from life.

Beyond, the horror froze her blood. Men and women were indistinguishable, for blades had chewed their flesh and snapped their bones and drowned the remnants in cooling blood. In a battered doorway upon a glistening spear a severed head hung agape, tongue ripped from its roots, eyes pulled from their cords, hair scythed from its scalp. On the bloody path a boned arm lay, a discarded glove, futile and forgotten. Draped over a low wall, a flayed forsaken body. Tossed into a ditch, a crushed heart. Pinned to a fence, the skull-less head of a mortal child. This was the aftermath of a hunt more brutal than any Rathgithr could recall, the remains rent thus, so each spectral warrior would have a token of the body from which he had ripped the soul.

The foetid air of fear choked her. The screams of the stolen souls chilled her. She had to get out. She knew not where she would run, for the eight other worlds were clearer now, nearer, and she knew the Devourers came from the south with their blades of flame. She knew that time here in the Midgard was ended. Fire, ice and chaos would now take them into the void. Stumbling in the darkness, lost, affrighted, she tumbled over a mortal girl child, whole but gravely wounded, by the embers of a dying fire. Her rapid, shallow breaths were as thunder in this pillaged barrow.

"I'm afraid of the dark," the child whispered, "and I can't find my mummy. She said to hide from the monsters only it was too dark. I'm so tired. Will you stay with me until I fall asleep? I'm afraid of the dark."

Rathgithr held back her sobs no longer, wanting to ease the child's fear yet unable to weave a lie that would do so. Instead, she pulled off her armour and cradled the small body in her arms, rocking gently from the strain of finding lost words, hoping the beating of her own heart was comfort enough. It was almost a relief to Rathgithr when the child's eyes finally closed.

Almost a relief. Until the lights went out.

Love Is a Stranger

Nick Walters

Kevin hated Valentine's Day. It loomed on his mental horizon, worse even than the prospect of exams. The Saturday before, he took the bus and mooched around Yate Shopping Centre, Parka done up right to his chin, Walkman on, his Eurythmics mixtape providing the soundtrack. The music isolated him from his surroundings, accentuating his feelings of alienation, yet providing comfort. I am not like them, Kevin thought, eying the crowds of shoppers: the mums with prams, the little kids, the beige and drab OAPs that thronged around the frosty flagstones and red brick passageways. I am special.

But not special enough to have ever received a Valentine's card.

The track finished. The next one began: *Love Is A Stranger.* One of his favourites. How Kevin longed to be tempted, to be driven far away. He slinked past Halfords. How Kevin longed to feel the passion that Annie Lennox sang about. He hesitated outside Top Man. How he longed for love, however dangerous, however destructive. He gazed up at the sightless eyes of a mannequin modelling the latest designer jacket and thin leather tie. His own pale reflection stared back at him. Parka. Cords. Cheap daps. Was there the flicker of a contemptuous smile around the mannequin's mouth? He wouldn't blame it.

Kevin turned away, towards the central square with its rectangular concrete pond of slimy water and bizarre sculpture which looked to him like a bunch of mutant alien bananas. Beyond it - Woolworths. Kevin gazed at the glass expanse of the shop front, a sour feeling percolating in his guts, but he found himself moving towards it, his daps scuffing the flagstones. Woolies, home of Pick'n'Mix. Woolies, where he'd bought his first Eurythmics album. Woolies, who sold greetings cards.

The sour feeling coalesced into a hard ball of distaste. Kevin shoved through the door and slunk past the Pick'n'Mix, resenting it for reminding him of happier, more innocent times. He hesitated by the records and tapes, idly fingering the new Thompson Twins single, then moved on, *Here Comes The Rain* Again filling his head.

He came to the cards. What was he doing here? He glanced with distaste up and down the racks of garish, overpriced, insincere rubbish. What a waste of money. He found himself in front of the Valentine's Cards. He picked one up, grimacing at the mawkish illustration of two cartoon bears hugging under a heart-shaped moon. He scanned the rhyme inside, its trite banality causing his lip to curl in a sneer. He was glad he had never received such a thing. He wouldn't want to go out with anyone who liked such tat.

Kevin moved on down the aisle. Here were more tasteful cards, illustrated with greater restraint. He picked one up. It was jet black, with a single red heart embossed in the centre. It looked illicit, forbidden. Inside it was blank, for the lover to pen their own message to their Valentine. Kevin smiled. He wouldn't mind receiving card like this! The person who sent this would be intelligent, sensual, dangerous even. His smile faded. He never had received a card like this, and he never would.

He was about to replace the card on its rack when his Walkman headphones were snatched from his head to dangle with a clatter against the back of his Parka. Here Comes The Rain Again was replaced by snorts of derisive laughter..

"Buyin' a Valentine's card, are we?"

"You ain't gotta girlfriend, you virgin!"

Kevin swung round. Two upper year boys towered over him, and not just any two; the worst two. Shane "Gyppo" Gypshayes and Craig "Dolly" Dolcoath.

Gyppo shoved him and he staggered back against the cards. He looked desperately around for shop assistants but there were none to be seen.

"I... I have got a girlfriend!" Kevin blurted out.

The two lads hooted with laughter.

"Whaaat, you prannock?! Boyfriend, you mean!" Shane Gypshayes was tall and broad, with glossy black hair, thick eyebrows and piercing blue eyes that seemed to look at the world with a permanent expression of raging contempt.

"He means his right hand," added Dolly, making the appropriate gesture. Dolly was small, pudgy, ginger and spotty, with National Health specs and breath that stank of cheesy Wotsits. Cruelty to animals was his bag. And cruelty to boys like Kevin.

"Sad little worm," snarled Gyppo.

Kevin straightened up, still clutching the card. "I have!" he shouted, and then, more calmly, "I have got a girlfriend." Somehow, saying the words calmed him, soothed him, made him feel strong, as if they were magically true.

"Rubbish!" snorted Dolly.

Gyppo grinned a predatory grin. "What's her name then?"

"Ann... " Kevin realised that he was wearing a Eurythmics T-shirt, albeit beneath his Parka, and the tinny strains of *Here Comes The Rain Again* could be heard - just about - emanating from his dangling headphones. "Er, Annalise."

"You're makin it up!" Gyppo shoved him again. Kevin staggered, but regained his balance. Gyppo glowered down at him. "You lyin' worm. You're a virgin and you'll die a virgin."

Kevin met his gaze unblinkingly. "Her name is Annalise." Amazed at his own bravery, he shoved past the two older lads and approached the till. His hands shook as he handed over the money (75p for a little piece of card!) and he blushed as Shane Gypshayes and Craig Dolcoath swaggered past him and out of Woolies, waving their fists in the air and chanting "Virgin! Virgin! Virgin!" at the tops of their voices.

Kevin couldn't meet the shop assistant's eye and was glad to be out of the shop and in the refreshing cold of the February air, holding the crinkly placky bag containing the card. He glanced around nervously for Gyppo and Dolly, but the two bullies were nowhere to be seen. Probably found someone or something else to torment, he thought with relief.

As he gazed around the square, he noticed a pale figure standing across the way, beyond the concrete pond. A girl, of about his own age, leaning against the column of brick between Boots and Halfords, arms folded, regarding him coolly and critically, a faint smile playing across her lips. She seemed under-dressed for the weather: white jeans, white daps, and a white t-shirt with a green and pink squiggle on it, over which she wore a short stonewashed blue denim jacket, sleeves rolled up despite the chilly air. She had short-cropped hair, just like Annie Lennox's, only it was dark, almost black. She was thin, and her face was very pale, almost as white as her jeans, and she wore pink lipstick and blue eyeshadow.

Kevin could not help himself. He stared. Even from this distance, she was heart-burstingly, gloriously beautiful. He felt something shift inside himself, as if a part of him that he never even knew about had just come alive. As he stared, gob-smacked, her smile widened, and she took a step towards him.

Kevin was about to move toward her when his upper left arm was seized in a painfully tight grip.

"Still got your Valentine's card, lovey?" hissed a hateful voice in his ear.

Kevin found himself being manhandled into the alleyway between Woolies and Tesco, his daps ineffectually scuffing the flagstones. He felt a shove in the small of his back and staggered into the service area behind the shops, a brutal, enclosed square of concrete, stacked with crates and giant metal bins on wheels.

There was no way out other than the way he'd been bundled in – and that was blocked by the forms of Shane Gypshayes and Craig Dolcoath. Kevin's knees began to tremble in fear.

Gyppo shoved him back against the bins. Dolly had snatched the placky bag and had found the card, which he held aloft with a cackling crow of triumph.

Gyppo's face was grim and hostile. "So you have. You better write it then, turd." He snatched Kevin's duffel bag and, Dolly holding him down, emptied its contents onto the oily, gritty concrete. Then he yanked the Walkman from Kevin's Parka pocket and, to his absolute horror, threw it to the ground. The plastic tape machine burst open, dislodging the cassette within. Then Gyppo stamped on it, crunching it into a shattered mess of useless plastic.

Tears sprang to Kevin's eyes. "Hey!" He struggled to free himself from Dolly's grip but the boy was too strong. The smell of cheesy Wotsits invaded his nostrils.

Gyppo was now rooting through the spilled contents of Kevin's duffel bag. He found a pen and held it aloft with a grunt of satisfaction. "Write!" he bellowed.

Dolly forced Kevin to his knees and he winced as his kneecaps struck the cold concrete. The card was slapped down before him and Gyppo shoved the pen into his face.

"Write!" shouted Gyppo again. "Write, worm!"

Hand shaking, Kevin took the pen. He could hardly see through tears.

"What did you say her name was?" demanded Gyppo.

"Annalise," said Kevin miserably. Why had he made up such a thing? This was all his own fault.

"Annalise!" sneered Dolly in his ear.

Gyppo's swarthy face was mirthless, joyless. "Anal Lice more like. Go on, write, 'To my darling Anal Lice from your secret admirer.'."

Dolly laughed, twisted his arm and hissed, "Write it!"

Sobbing, Kevin wrote in a shaky hand, with some difficulty, "To my darling Annalise from your secret admirer."

When Gyppo saw what he had written, he snatched the pen away and hurled it clattering against brick. "I said write 'Anal Lice,' you flid!" he roared. Kevin felt his ears gripped by stubby fingers and he yelped in agony as Dolly hauled him to his feet. He caught a wild glimpse of Gyppo's reddened face contorted in anger. A fist hit his stomach and he went down, winded, gasping for air. His heart felt as though it was about to burst. He was hauled up again – by the arms thankfully – and spun around, assailed by punches and kicks, shouts and jeers. He stumbled over his own feet, arms raised, trying to shield himself. His arm was seized – Gyppo – and he was swung around, head first, towards the dull grey flank of one of the metal bins. He opened his mouth to scream but there wasn't time. There was an immense impact, an explosion of pain, a flash of blinding white light, and then nothing.

***

When Kevin came to, it was to find the pale girl from the square standing looking down at him. Close up, her face was intensely striking, the pink lipstick and blue eyeshadow standing out in stark contrast against her pallid skin. Her blue eyes were like jewels and her gelled hair glistened in the dull February daylight.

Kevin groaned. His head throbbed fit to split. He tried to stand, but waves of pain lanced through his skull and he fell back against the bin. He blinked up at the girl. She stared back down at him. She looked amused, curious.

Her gaze shifted slightly. "Ooh, is this for me?" She picked up the card.

"Urrrgh," was all Kevin could manage to say. More pain throbbed in his head and he squeezed his eyes shut in an effort to shut it out. When he opened them again, the girl was gone.

Kevin staggered painfully to his feet. His possessions lay strewn all around the service area. He retrieved them and replaced them in his duffel bag, except for the smashed Walkman, the remains of which he chucked into one of the metal bins with a sniff of sorrow. How he'd explain that to his parents, he didn't know. It had been a birthday present and one of his most treasured possessions. He was hardly ever to be seen without it. Hatred for Gyppo and Dolly surged through him like wildfire. But what could puny he do against mighty them?

The girl. The girl! Kevin ran from the service area, his head throbbing, and back out to the square. "Annalise!" he called. He didn't know why, but somehow, he knew that was her name, as if he had conjured her into existence. He ran around the concrete pool to where he had first seen her leaning nonchalantly against the wall. He ran down every alleyway of Yate shopping centre. He even swallowed his embarrassment and slipped into Etam for a furtive look around. But wherever he searched, the girl in white, Annalise, was nowhere to be found. In the end he got the bus back home; fish fingers and chips for tea the only thing to look forward to.

***

The dreaded day, Valentine's Day, passed without incident, and without card – as always . His sisters Judith and Evelyn (one older, one younger) got loads, as usual, and teased him mercilessly about his lack of cards – also as usual. Dad had been predictably and justifiably angry about the Walkman (Kevin had said he'd dropped it), and said that Kevin would have to save up to buy a replacement because he was damned if he was going to fork out for a new one.

School was the usual that week; enjoyment of English and endurance of Games, and avoidance of Gyppo and Dolly. The upper year boys, however, left him alone, even on Valentine's day itself when he'd dreaded they would bring up the subject of the card and Annalise. Perhaps they thought he'd been punished enough. Whatever the reason, he was glad of it, though he still cowered when Gyppo or Dolly shoved past him in the dinner queue.

All week, his thoughts revolved around Annalise. Who was she? She certainly wasn't at Mangotsfield. She must be at another school. He had no idea of how to even begin finding out. He began to doubt that he'd ever actually seen her, especially as he'd lain dazed by the bins. Had he imagined the whole thing? Had his loneliness, fuelled by Eurythmics songs, created an hallucination? But the card had gone – he'd looked for it as he'd gathered up his possessions – so Annalise must have taken it. Therefore, she must be real.

Thank God that – although it had resulted in a beating – he had not written 'Anal lice' as Gyppo had told him to.

The only plan Kevin could come up with was to re-visit the scene. Go back to Yate shopping centre, see if he could find Annalise. And so, that Saturday saw him back on the bus, this time with no soundtrack for his journey, on the top deck barrelling down the country lanes towards Yate.

***

Kevin trudged round Yate Shopping Centre, his heart sinking with every corner he rounded. With no music to insulate himself from the outside world he felt vulnerable, exposed. And with no music to insulate himself from the inner world, negative thoughts flooded his mind. Fool! he told himself. Annalise didn't exist! And even if she did, she wouldn't be here. And even if she was here, she wouldn't want to talk to him. No girl did!

And then there she was, standing outside Woolies.

She still wore her white jeans, white daps, white t-shirt with the pink and green squiggles, and stonewash blue denim jacket with the sleeves rolled up. Her hair was still black and gelled, and she still wore pink lipstick and blue eyeshadow on her pale face. The same amused, curious expression.

She was standing in front of the plate glass window with its enormous garish SALE! signs, arms by her side, as if waiting for someone. Waiting for him?

Her beauty intimidated him and he almost turned and fled. But something deep inside made him go on, made him move through the crowds of shoppers, who didn't even seem to see the gorgeous vision in their midst, towards the girl. Towards Annalise.

Presently he was standing right in front of her. She was a little taller than him.

"H... Hello," he said.

"Hello!" she said brightly. She gave a little wave.

"Er... "

"Thanks for the card," she said. "Though I don't think it was meant for me. Who's Annalise?"

Kevin frowned in confusion. “No-one... ” He didn’t want to tell her about Gyppo and Dolly.

A look of concern caused her to narrow her eyes and incline her head. “Are you all right? You took quite a beating just now.”

“Just now? It was last week!”

The girl pouted. “Yes... of course it was... ” She looked confused. “Come on, let’s walk.” Without waiting for him, she strode off along East Walk.

He ran to catch up with her. “So what’s your name?”

“What’s yours?”

“Kevin.”

The girl who wasn’t called Annalise pouted. “I had a brother called that.”

She walked quickly and Kevin struggled to keep up. “Had? Is he... is he dead?”

The girl shook her head brusquely, angrily. “No... not him!”

Kevin frowned. Odd thing to say. “So what *is* your name?” His mind’s eye flicked through Eurythmics songs. “Belinda? Jennifer?”

The girl stopped walking, turned to him. Her eyes shone, as if she was about to cry. “Stephanie,” she said softly. “Stephanie Hindmarsh. Ring any bells?”

She seemed full of strange phrases and non-sequiturs .

“No... Stephanie.’

It was a beautiful name, a sexy name. He said so.

‘That’s a beautiful, sexy name.”

The girl’s – Stephanie’s – eyes widened. Her mouth formed an ‘O’ of surprise.

Oh God! Why did he have to say ‘sexy’? Fool!

“Sexy. Well.” She narrowed her ice-blue eyes. “Have you ever...?”

Kevin felt himself blushing. She was very frank, unnervingly forthright. His voice sounded small and far away.

“Well ... no, I’m only fifteen.”

"Neither have I. Had a few boyfriends, before ... but we just kissed." She sighed, a sound like a winter breeze. "Now I will never know the pleasures of the flesh."

That seemed unlikely, thought Kevin, gazing upon her stark beauty. "Why do you say that?"

She inclined her head again, as if weighing something up. "Because I am not made of flesh," she said softly.

Kevin couldn't think of anything to say. He swallowed. He blinked.

An ice-cream hand touched his. "I'm made of ectoplasm!"

Kevin snatched his hand back, as if he'd been burned. "Eh?"

Stephanie raised her arms in clear exasperation. "I'm a ghost, you idiot!"

Kevin felt the world sway around him. It was as though everything he'd ever known , ever learned, was a lie – hang on though, a ghost?! "Do me a favour!" he scoffed.

Without a word, Stephanie turned away from him and walked straight through the plate-glass window of Tesco. Seconds later she emerged from a brick wall further along East Walk, and drifted towards him, her white daps clearly a metre above the flagstones.

Stephanie alighted in front of him waggling her fingers in the air. She grinned broadly. "Woooooo!"

"You're a ghost," muttered Kevin lamely. He looked around in a stunned daze. "But no-one seemed to see you... do that."

"You're the only one who can see me, apparently," she said brightly.

"Why? Why me?"

Stephanie shrugged. "Dunno. You must be special, or something."

Kevin's heart swelled. He knew it! He knew he was special! Here before him was the living – well, the once-living – proof!

Stephanie began to walk again and he fell in beside her. He began to notice the other people looking at him oddly as he conversed with the ghost girl. Must look like he was talking to himself.

Stephanie was talking now. Babbling, even. "It's such a relief to actually meet someone who can see me! It's been a long, lonely time, stuck here. A year, haunting a shopping centre."

It was, Kevin admitted, an unlikely site for a haunting. Not your usual castle or stately home with its attendant spirits. "Why here?"

"It's the place I loved most when I was alive."

Kevin glanced around at the concrete and red brick. "What, here?"

"I was only fifteen when I died," she said reproachfully. "I was a pretty shallow girl. Pop music and shopping, that was about it. Never got the chance to develop into a full person."

"What did... how did... " Kevin struggled for the right words.

"Leukaemia," came the reply. "Change the subject! Music. Your favourite band?"

"Eurythmics," said Kevin automatically.

Stephanie gasped. "Me too! That's why I cut my hair short. One advantage of being dead, it'll never grow!"

Kevin was working it out. If she'd been dead a year, that meant February 1983. She would have had time to listen to *Sweet Dreams (Are Made Of This)*. "You know, they had a new album out last November, after... "

"After I died, yeah?" she said conversationally.

"Ahem, yeah... called *Touch*."

Stephanie stopped walking and turned to face him. "You realise this can't go anywhere, don't you? I'm a ghost, you're still alive. The least compatible couple ever."

"Doesn't matter," said Kevin. "What matters is how we feel." How he had the confidence to say the words, God alone knew. "And I feel that I was made able to see you for a reason."

Stephanie blinked. "Don't!"

He reached out and held her hand. It was ice cold, and tingled, like static electricity. "We're both lonely. That's why we've been brought together by God or whatever it is that's in charge of these things! We need each other."

Stephanie closed her eyes. “Oh, Kevin.”
“Stephanie.”
He leaned in and kissed her on the lips, tentatively, delicately. It felt like ice and fire and he felt as if he was flying through space as his arms enfolded her thin, dead body. He felt ghostly arms enfold him.
And then suddenly she was gone and he was left standing there in the middle of Yate shopping centre hugging air and attracting the puzzled looks of the Saturday shoppers.

***

The following week, Kevin floated through a dream. He had (at last!) been touched by love. The love of a dead person, yes, but it felt more real than anything else in his life. It made him special, made him able to endure everything: his father’s moods, his mother’s cooking, his sisters’ taunts and jeers. It didn’t matter if he never saw Stephanie again; that brief ghostly kiss, that spectral embrace, had been enough.
He would see her again though – he was sure of it. From the little she’d said about her existence in the afterlife, she was confined to the place she’d loved the most when she was alive: Yate Shopping Centre. He was the only living being able to perceive her, she was lonely; she needed him. They needed each other. How could she not be there?
And so he sailed through the week and if anyone noticed he was different, they didn’t say. His dad frowned at him once or twice, but that was all. How he longed to tell someone about Stephanie! But that way lay certain ridicule and the mental hospital. Stephanie was his, his alone, and she would stay that way forever.
Kevin’s new-found serenity even saw him through an encounter with his nemesis, Shane Gypshayes.
Wednesday afternoon. Just after lunch. The bell rang and everyone was rushing to get to their one o’clock classes. Kevin, head down, lost in daydreams about Stephanie, in the main corridor. A crush of bodies, shouting. The usual. Kevin squeezed through the double doors that led to the side corridor leading to the classrooms and found himself face to face with Shane Gypshayes.

Gyppo's eyes shone with tears. On seeing Kevin, he angrily wiped them away and barged past, emitting a strangled sob. Kevin stared dumbstruck at his retreating back.

"Don't you know?" Geraint Smith, a boy in his year said. "His Dad's in prison. His Mum drinks. Slaps him about a bit."

Kevin thought of his sometimes chaotic but comparatively idyllic home life. Before he knew it, he was running back up the main corridor after Gyppo. What Geraint had told him explained, but did not excuse, the way Shane was, but Kevin, touched by the love of Stephanie, felt an overwhelming surge of benevolence.

"Gyppo! Er, Shane!" he called.

Gyppo stumbled to a halt and turned around. The tears were gone. He glowered down at Kevin.

"I... I forgive you."

Gyppo's hands curled into fists. "Get lost, worm," he snarled.

Somewhat deflated, Kevin backed away. In an hour he'd forgotten all about the incident, lost again in daydreams of Stephanie.

***

Stephanie was there on Saturday as he'd expected, outside Woolies, like last time.

They hugged. It felt wonderful. The coldness of her body seeped right down into his bones and he was suffused with a delicious yet almost painful feeling of pins and needles all over his skin, from his feet right up to his scalp.

After minutes, hours, days? they disengaged. Several shoppers were staring at Kevin oddly. He ignored them.

They walked slowly hand in hand around the central square.

"Sorry for popping off like that just now," Stephanie began. "Got a bit carried away – can't control it sometimes."

"Control what?"

"Transference. I'm not always here," she said mysteriously. "Other times, I'm in... another domain."

"You mean heaven?"

She frowned. "Not religious, are you?"

Kevin thought of his R.E. lessons in which he was learning about the religions of the world. All seemed equally bizarre, equally unlikely. Or did they? Proof of life after death was standing right there beside him in white jeans and stonewash denim. But did any religion speak of ghosts? "Not particularly."

"Good. Well, no, not 'heaven', that's just a word people have for it. 'Astral plane' is more accurate. All ghosts end up there. It's wonderful!" She smiled at him. "But I prefer it down here. With you."

"You said you popped off 'just now' when it was last week..."

Stephanie folded her arms. "Is our relationship going to consist solely of me explaining the rules of the afterlife to you?"

"No, but come on! Wouldn't you be curious?"

She inclined her head. "Suppose. Well, time doesn't exist on the astral plane. It's all one big moment. From my point of view, it's only just now since we last met." She frowned. "It doesn't quite work like that but I can't see any other way to explain it."

They turned out of the square along East Walk.

"You say you were a shallow, fifteen-year-old girl when you were alive but you don't speak like one."

"I've spent a year hob-nobbing with Jane Austen, George Orwell, Emmeline Pankhurst and Sid Vicious. Amongst others. I've grown up rather a bit."

Kevin's mind boggled. He wanted to ask more but could see that Stephanie was getting restless.

"Come on, let's have some fun!" she said, grinning maliciously.

And so they did. They spent a pleasant afternoon pranking shoppers. Stephanie, invisible to them, would knock items from shelves, or move their shopping trolleys whilst they weren't looking. Local news would later report on 'poltergeist activity' in Woolies and a priest would be called in to bless the place, whilst Stephanie looked on, laughing.

Later that afternoon, they sat on a bench at the end of North Walk. Here, a wide strip of dirty grass separated them from the busy B4059, which took the traffic past the White Lion pub and around the periphery of the shopping centre.

"Sweet dreams are made of this," said Kevin.

Stephanie laughed. They kissed.

They sat holding hands for a while. A wistful look played across Stephanie's pale face as she stared at the expanse of muddy grass. "This is it. The boundary of my domain. I can go no further."

"What happens if you try?"

"This." She stood up abruptly and walked out onto the grass. Kevin observed that her feet did not disturb a single blade. A few metres in, she stopped, and turned to face him, smiling wanly. He went to stand beside her.

Thoughts of taking her home played across his mind. "You can't go any further?"

Stephanie shook her head. "No, this is it." She frowned as he took her arm and gently tried to lead her further out. "Don't try to make me, it hurts!"

"Sorry, sorry!"

They went back to sit on the bench, and held each other for a while. In the end, it was Kevin who had to pop off, as he had to be home for his tea of liver and onions.

"That's another advantage of being dead, not having to eat my Mum's cooking," he said.

He waved at Stephanie from the top deck of the bus as she stood by the bench at the edge of her earthly domain, waving forlornly back at him. He didn't care what the other passengers thought. Let him be the nutter on the bus.

***

Kevin met Stephanie every Saturday from then on, as winter slowly gave way to spring, and the Easter holidays began to loom. Two weeks off school – two weeks in which Kevin planned to spend as much time in the company of his ghostly girlfriend as possible.

But it was not to be.

***

It was the last Saturday before the Easter holidays. Stephanie was waiting outside Woolies as was their custom, but as Kevin approached her, he could see there was something different about her. Her usual, beautiful, curious smile was gone, replaced by a serious, withdrawn expression.

They did the usual things: hugging, kissing, holding hands, pranking shoppers, but he could tell that Stephanie's spectral heart wasn't in it.

They ended up on their 'Sweet Dreams' bench at the end of North Walk, just holding hands. He'd got used to the cold, fizzy feel of her ectoplasm.

At length she said it, said the words he was dreading to hear, but somehow knew she was going to say.

"I've got to go."

Kevin didn't speak, just stared at the grass. There were daisies now, spots of bright yellow and white amidst the green. "Go where?"

"To the astral plane." She let go of him, put her head in her hands. "It's hard to explain – we ghosts only have limited exposure on this plane, unless we're trapped here or have unfinished business. Then we have to move on. The astral plane has to claim us, eventually."

"But I'm unfinished business!" wailed Kevin desperately.

Stephanie shook her head. "Not in the right way. You were not – connected to me whilst I lived. You did not murder me. I just died of a disease, I have nothing to avenge. No-one to haunt! So I've got to go."

Kevin wanted to be grown up about this, but the tears came, hot and fast. "I don't want you to go!" he blubbered. He dashed the tears away angrily with his sleeve.

"I don't want to go either," said Stephanie softly. "But it can't be helped."

A bus trundled along the road past the White Lion, full of passengers bound for Bristol. Kevin stood up. "I'm gonna kill myself so we can be together!"

He started to run but a cold hand gripped his. “It doesn’t work like that!”

Kevin tore himself free. If he ran out on to the grass, he’d pass the point of no return for Stephanie, and she wouldn’t be able to stop him. He ran a short way then stopped. He sank to his knees, lost amidst the grass and daisies. There was no way he could kill himself, he knew that. He was too scared. Mutely, he picked himself up and sat down on the bench.

“Your ghost would be attached to the place you love most,” Stephanie was saying. “Which I doubt would be this place. So we would not be together.”

“It is this place! I love this place, because of you!” Kevin sniffed.

“Even so, I don’t want you to die! You’re a nice boy. A good person. You’ll find someone, a living girl, who can love you properly, in ways that I never can.”

Kevin was losing it again. His nose was running. He blew it into his hanky. “I don’t care! I don’t want anyone else. I want you!”

“I told you it could never work between us!”

Kevin shoved the hanky back into his pocket. “Don’t say that.”

They sat in silence together for a while, holding hands. Then Stephanie stood up. Her eyes were shining. “It’s time.”

They hugged for the last time.

They kissed for the last time.

“I’ve got something for you,” Stephanie whispered in his ear.

Kevin found a small cardboard box pressed into his hand. He looked at it, blinking. It was a Walkman – one of the new models with noise reduction and a graphic equaliser. “How the hell...?”

“I’m a ghost, dummy! Nicking stuff is easy!”

Kevin slid the box into the inside pocket of his anorak. He smiled through his tears. “Thanks.”

Stephanie inclined her head. “It was the least I could do.”

“So this is goodbye?”

Stephanie nodded. She was already beginning to look insubstantial. He could see the traffic through her. For the very first time, she actually looked like a ghost.

A huge sense of desolation enfolded Kevin. There was nothing he could do to stop this. "I love you."

Stephanie faded further into nothingness. "I love you too," she said, her voice nothing more than an icy whisper. She smiled, gave him the thumbs-up, and then was gone, suddenly and shockingly, as if someone had switched her off.

Kevin stood there for an eternity, and then turned and strode stiffly back along North Walk into Yate shopping centre, not caring who saw his tears, who thought him mad.

Stephanie was gone.

He would never see her again.

Once more, he was totally alone.

About the Authors

Margaret Carruthers has lived in Filton, Bristol for 40 years with her husband. They share their house with a cat and two chickens. They have a son who has moved to Germany. After retiring, she spends her free time reading all kinds of fiction from fantasy to crime. She joined North Bristol Writers two years ago and enjoys writing fiction ranging from fantasy to horror to crime. Her first novel is available on Kindle.

Roz Clarke resides in a hidden corner of North Bristol, deep in the long grass. She's a freelance writer and editor, and a graduate of the MMU Creative Writing MA and of Clarion West. She's a guest editor at Kristell Ink, has had short stories published in various magazines and anthologies and is a co-editor of the anthologies *Colinthology, Airship Shape & Bristol Fashion* and *Fight Like a Girl,* alongside Joanne Hall. She's been a member of the BristolCon committee since its inception in 2009, and is delighted to have come to rest in that peculiar, inspiring city. Roz blogs occasionally at www.firefew.com and you can tweet her at @zora_db.

Clare Dornan is a tv director by day, and a writer of short stories by night. She's published in the North Bristol Writers anthology *North by SouthWest* and has performed her stories in pubs and festivals around Bristol. She has a ridiculously low fear threshold and can only write ghost stories, with the lights on, locked in the safest of places.

Desiree Fischer is a writer who lives in Bristol. She is originally from a small town in south-west Germany, but she knew from approximately the age of five that she wanted to live in England. She enjoys the challenge of writing in a language that's not her mother tongue and while her writing focuses mainly on science fiction and fantasy, she isn't averse to trying her hand at other genres. She had her first story published in *North by SouthWest.*

Dolly Garland writes fantasy that is a bit like her – muddled in cultures. Having lived in three countries, and several cities, she now calls London her home, although the roots of her fantasy have returned to India, where she grew up. You can chat to her @DollyGarland on Twitter, @DollyGarlandAuthor on Facebook, and www.dollygarland.com.

Chrissey Harrison is a writer of all kinds of escapist fiction; mish-mashes of science-fiction, fantasy, horror and romance in various proportions. She has published her own and other writer's works under Great Escape Publishing, including the novelette 'The Star Cain Prophecy' and short fiction anthology *Great Escapes: Volume 1.* You can find lots of Chrissey's micro fiction, flash fiction and short stories at thegreatesc.com and on her blog. Her short story 'The Collective' features in Hellbound Media's graphic horror anthology *Shock Value Green.* She is currently working on her first novel, supernatural thriller *Mime,* which will tie in to the growing mixed media world of Gabriel Cushing. Chrissey has been involved with Gabriel's on-screen adventures from the beginning, as a producer and special effects artist. Also an avid crafter and creator of things (props, costumes, cuddly toys, geeky accessories etc.), when she's not writing or film making you'll often find her hunched over a sewing machine or getting into a sticky mess with glue. Owner of 15-year-old goldfish Hope, Dignity and Ambition, who have their own twitter account @acquariumdays.

Kevlin Henney writes shorts and flashes and drabbles of fiction and books and articles on software development. His fiction has appeared online and on tree (*Litro, New Scientist, Physics World, LabLit, The Pygmy Giant, The Fabulist, The Spec Fiction Hub, 365 Tomorrows* and others) and has been included in a number of anthologies (*North* *by Southwest, We Can Improve You, Haunted, The Salt Anthology of New Writing 2013, A Box of Stars Beneath the Bed, Eating My Words, Scraps, Jawbreakers* and others). As well as having his work rejected and make no impression whatsoever on writing competitions, Kevlin's stories have been longlisted, shortlisted and placed. He won the Crimefest 2014 Flashbang contest and was a finalist in the NYC Midnight Short Story Challenge 2016. He reads at spoken word events, winning the National Flash-Fiction Day Oxford flash slam in 2012, and has performed his work on local radio (BBC Radio Bristol and Ujima). Kevlin organises the BristolFlash events for National Flash-Fiction Day and the Bristol Festival of Literature. He lives in Bristol and online. He can be read on his blog at http://asemantic.net and stalked on twitter as @KevlinHenney.

During the day **Maria Herring** is a perfectly normal English Literature and Language teacher, but after 3:30pm she lets her sff geek out. So far, that's got her two published novels (*Legacy of a Warrior Queen* and *The Book of Revelations* – both available on Amazon), a bunch of short stories, some of which won prizes from Dark Tales Magazine and the Writer's Village, plus an Aeon Awards short-listing. Having shared her love of the English language around China and France for the past decade, she's finally back in Bristol working on her third novel, *Dawn of Darkness*, mentored by acclaimed sff novelist Liz Williams, while still writing those peculiar short stories. She's a proud member of the North Bristol Writers group, has a fat tabby cat and is addicted to tea. She honestly does have friends. (www.facebook.com/MariaHerringAuthor)

Ian McConaghy is a Bristol-based artist exploring the interface between the visual and the narrative. He has created several graphic stories while being a member of the North Bristol Writers and the book cover design for

The Dark Half of the Year. He is a published illustrator of educational material. He is currently working on his next exhibition, which will explore intelligent buildings, genetic engineering, cryogenics and artificial intelligence. The exhibition will be a multi-media platform mixing images, sound and words. The initial digital artwork has already generated ideas for his first novel, set in a dystopian near future. (www.thesilentroom.co.uk)

Suzanne McConaghy is a modern linguist turned full-time writer. She has published over a dozen works and courses in the languages field, most recently, a series of stories in Spanish and French for teenagers. She has written a middle-grade fantasy adventure novel (in English!) which is currently out to agents and has begun a dystopian YA novel. She participates in writing short fiction and particularly enjoys reading stories at events in and around Bristol.

Madeleine Meyjes is 19 and currently living in Northern California. She writes poems and short stories in her spare time and blogs about the San Francisco music scene.

Ian Millsted's short story 'House Blood' was given an honourable mention in Ellen Datlow's *Best New Horror 8* and he's had stories published in the anthologies *Airship Shape and Bristol Fashion, Challenger Unbound, Colinthology* and elsewhere. His novel *Silence Rides Alone* was published by Sundown Press in 2016 and his non-fiction book about *Doctor Who, Black Archives 8: Black Orchid* was released by Obverse Books, also in 2016.

Justin Newland writes historical, fantasy and speculative fiction with a supernatural bent. For further author info, see www.justinnewland.com. Short stories in anthologies include: *'The Fool of Abbot's Leigh'* in Hidden Bristol and *'Fisher of Men'* in North by Southwest (both Tangent Books). He's a regular panellist at BristolCon and reader during events in the Bristol Festival of Literature. His first novel, *The Genes of Isis,* is to be published by Silverwood Books in early 2016. For more info, see www.thegenesofisis.com. He is currently working on a fantasy novel set in Ming Dynasty China, entitled 'The Old Dragon's Head'. And yes, of course it features dragons.

Thomas David Parker was born in Bristol, but was quickly exiled to the Forest of Dean so his childhood could be shaped into an Enid Blyton novel. From a young age, he discovered a joy of stories and was drawn to the realms of fantasy and the supernatural. His earliest influence was Terry Pratchett, who was later joined by Neil Gaiman and M. R. James. He currently lives in a 17th century pub, where he spends his time writing short stories and terrifying his mother that he'll never settle down. He is a member of the Stokes Croft Writers and co-host of Talking Tales, a bi-monthly podcast and local storytelling event.

Arriving in Bristol by way of London, Coventry, Cambridge, Glastonbury and Bath, **M E Rodman** has had short stories published in the anthology *Airship Shape and Bristol Fashion* and the Australian short story collection *A Picture's Worth* as well as book reviews in *Vector, Prism* and the thebookbag.com and poetry in *Girl2Girl*, a multimedia anthology. A debut novel *Blood and Thorn* is currently with the publishers.

Ken Shinn still lives in Bristol with his two cats and too much beer in his fridge. He still loves fantastic fiction of all forms but horror, in particular. Other horror stories of his can be found in the anthologies *Teeming Terrors, Killer Bees from Outer Space, Weird Ales* and *Tales from the Damned*. He is also still working on turning his steampunk short story 'Case of the Vapours' into a full novel, hopefully to be completed and published within the next twelve months, and whatever other writing assignments he can fit in around his job with the NHS. Oh, and he's very fond of haggis.

Peter Sutton has a not so secret lair in the wilds of Fishponds, Bristol and dreams up stories, many of which are about magpies. He's the author of *A Tiding of Magpies* and the novel *Sick City Syndrome* (both from Kensington Gore Press). You can find him all over social media or worrying about events he's organised at the Bristol Festival of Literature. On Twitter he's @suttope and his Bristol Book Blog is http://brsbkblg.blogspot.co.uk/ and his website is http://petesutton.com/ He's contributing editor of *Far Horizons* e-magazine (https://farhorizonsmagazine.wordpress.com/ .

Nick Walters is the author of five and a half Doctor Who novels including the *Doctor Who Magazine* award-winning *Reckless Engineering*. He has also written numerous SF and horror short stories. He is the author of *Mutually Assured Domination,* the recent novel in the Lethbridge-Stewart series from Candy Jar Books. He lives in Bristol with his bike and his cat, his favourite band is The Fall, and his favourite Doctor is Tom Baker.

Acknowledgments

North Bristol Writers would like to express their thanks to the following people for helping this book to become a reality.

Cavan Scott for taking time out of his busy schedule to write the introduction.

Ian McConaghy for the cover art and design.

Ian Millsted for commissioning and Peter Sutton for principal editing. Ana Marija Meshkova for typesetting. Suzanne McConaghy for proof reading, with an assist from Maria Herring.

We would also like to thank Bristolcon Foundation for all the support it has given the writing group for the past couple of years and The Inn on the Green for giving us a home every other Thursday. Also, Arnos Vale Cemetery for hosting an event at which a number of these stories received their first public performance.

North Bristol Writers would also like to thank City Art Gallery, Claire Fisher, Bethan Millsted, Elizabeth Millsted, Carolyn Morris, Rose Orr, Alisha Ramsey and Donald and his troosers.

Lightning Source UK Ltd.
Milton Keynes UK
UKOW01f1751280917
310070UK00007B/306/P

9 780955 418228